Backbeats and

Innocence

Terry D.
Newberry

Cookie —
with love —
Terry

Backbeats and

Innocence

Terry D. Newberry

www.terrynewberry.com

A collection of short stories from the

heart... for the heart.

TERRY D. NEWBERRY

PSALM/**one** PRESS

Published by

PSALM/ one PRESS

Atlanta, Georgia

Cover Design by Michael Scarano
Copy Editing by Patricia Ann Babb
Printed and bound by Rocky Heights Binding
Library of Congress Cataloging-in-Publication Data
Newberry, Terry D.
Backbeats and Innocence
Stories from the heart… for the heart.

1st Edition

ISBN 978-1-7370707-0-2
Available in E-Book

Also By **Terry D. Newberry**

No Average Joe

The Boss

Almost There

For Ezra and Jude -

My prayer is that your lives will be as blessed, rich and full as mine has been.

And for my muse. Always.

Backbeats and Innocence

TABLE OF CONTENTS

FIREFLIES

Peace. What a lovely word.

Peace has been in short supply of late. It has been crowded out by angry voices and bitter rhetoric, by screams and chants and blame. It has been shattered like a fine crystal vase dropped from a rooftop.

It's been a hard year for all of us. Killer viruses gave way to anarchy and blood running in our streets; violence and madness and death and mayhem coming in wave after wave – it is hard to wrap our minds around the magnitude of the anger.

Then even the ocean sent its own destructive emissary as if it too wanted to have a voice in the cacophony.

It feels like someone unlocked the hasp of some ancient lockbox and released restless and unruly spirits on to our unsuspecting world.

And I'll tell you straight – the last few months have taken a toll on us. All of us. Everyone. Individually, collectively, as a people, as a nation, as a planet. Brotherhoods and relationships that took decades to forge seemed to fall apart overnight. The hard work and building, the sacrifice of the martyred – all of it seemingly ground up in the inexorable wave of passion that cast a *film noir* of fear and hatred over us.

The world seems to be crumbling before our very eyes.

I love to spend time on our patio. Our home is surrounded by woods and there is a gentle creek that paints its music on the air as it tumbles and gurgles its way through the rocks.

Every year there are fireflies. They show up in early summer like some gypsy dance troupe, hang around for a few days, and then head off to the next stop on the tour.

During the few days of their engagement in our woods, I sit on my patio and watch in joy as they dance their aerial acrobatics.

But not this year.

This year, it seemed they watched the news and decided to stay wherever it is that fireflies go to wait out times of insanity. Night after night I sat on the patio, watching the dark forest for a spark or two.

Night after night I went inside disappointed.

Perhaps you'll think I'm silly, but I need to confess something to you. I have been praying for the fireflies to come. I needed to see them, to be reminded of the purity of God and His simple love for us. I needed to see their carefree ballet executed on the night currents. I needed to be reminded about the things that matter.

You see, I believe my heavenly Dad loves me and is concerned with even the tiniest things in my life. Nothing escapes His attention.

So, I prayed. I told Him about the darkness in our world. I told Him about the fear that has etched itself into the faces I see in the marketplace. I told Him about the suspicion I see in the eyes of those I pass in the streets. I told Him we needed Him now more than ever. I told Him I was anxious. I asked Him to send the fireflies.

And then I waited.

Tonight, I sat on the patio, surrounded by the sounds of a summer evening. The golden light of the gloaming slowly gave way to the blues and purples of twilight. As if on cue, the night creatures began to tune up. Cicadas readied up their wings, frogs gurgled and croaked, and the owls hooted. The orchestra was ready for the evening.

And then something magical happened. The fireflies showed up. A single blink in the dark forest. Then another. And another.

The nocturnal orchestra accompanied them as they performed their now-you-see-me-now-you-don't routine. Here one minute, gone the next.

They flew a mission of loop-the-loops on the night breeze and brought their own special magic to the twilight as it slowly faded into night. They stitched patterns in the darkness and created a tapestry of peace that slowly washed over me.

And I watched in joy because I knew that God heard my silly little prayer.

He hears yours too.

Try Him. Test Him. Go pray for some fireflies to show up.

GRACE

When my girls were younger, my daughter Amanda received $100 for her birthday. Excited, she talked her mom into a shopping trip to spend her birthday cash.

Happily, they shopped for a few hours, carefully picking out each dreamed-about item and storing it in the shopping cart. The treasure trove grew and grew, and Amanda became more excited with each new addition to the growing pile.

Finally, they made their way to the register and began to unload the carefully selected items. One by one the scanner registered the price as Amanda eagerly watched, dreaming of getting home with her new-found prizes and proud to pay for it all by herself.

At last, the total was presented and she reached into her little purse to find her birthday stash.

It wasn't there. Carefully she checked each corner of the purse. Nothing. She dug through each of her pockets. Still nothing. A little frantic now, she checked her mom's purse and her pockets.

Nothing. Just nothing.

Finally, in shame, she told the cashier that she must have lost her money. The cashier made an announcement and pretty soon folks all over the store were looking for a lost $100 bill to return to my tearful daughter.

Her mom helped her search the store and everywhere they had been, but there were no $100 bills to be seen.

When they arrived home, I asked what she bought. She burst into tears. Through sniffles and sobs, she explained what happened.

As her Daddy I wanted to pull out my wallet and give her a crisp $100 bill to replace the one she had lost.

But the Father in me recognized that this was an opportunity to teach her responsibility. So, I explained the importance of keeping up with money and hoped this financial lesson would stick and not be washed away by the still-flowing tears of my heartbroken little girl.

The following Sunday I shared this story with my Bible study class, explaining that sometimes God allows us to learn responsibility from our experiences. Seemed like a fair point at the time.

The very next day, envelopes with no return address began to arrive at our house. Each was addressed to Amanda, and each one she opened contained cash. Bills of all denominations spilled onto the table as she opened the envelopes.

Well, to make a long story short, Amanda wound up with $200 to replace the $100 that she had lost.

So, dutiful teacher that I am, I shared the "rest of the story" with my class the following Sunday, knowing beyond all doubt that they were the culprits behind the mysterious envelopes.

They just listened and smiled their Mona Lisa smiles, knowing something that I didn't know.

They are wiser than I am, you see. They understood that I wanted to teach Amanda responsibility, but they taught her grace instead.

As it turned out, she liked grace a lot better.

Don't we all?

THE TABLE

The birthday cake sits in the middle of the table. And in the middle of the cake, stuck in what seems to be a couple acres of icing, there is a single candle. The flame wavers and gleams in the air.

Now please understand, this isn't just any cake – no sir. This is the cake of cakes, the chosen, the *Pièce De Résistance* of cakes – a genuine birthday cake from Pollman's bakery. You know, the famous round cake with the tasty lemon filling between the layers.

"Happy Birthday Mom" is written in icing script across the top. There are roses made of pure sugar; red and pink, all over the cake. A single one of those roses could put you into a diabetic coma, let me tell you. Trust me, I know from experience.

We sit around the old kitchen table, friends and family, on this special occasion. We are celebrating Nan's birthday, another trip around the sun. And that is always a special day. But today it is even more special. Because we are celebrating at the kitchen table in MeMaw's house.

I remember the first time I sat at that table. I was just a kid, maybe 15 or so, visiting the family on some business that I have long since forgotten. I knocked on the door (the back door - only dweebs and vacuum cleaner salesmen knocked on the front door) and MeMaw let me in. Of course, she wasn't MeMaw back then, she was just Mrs. Gillis. You know, Lum's wife. Mother to Diane and Betty.

She let me in and there sat the entire family around the table. MeMaw offered me coffee and pie. Never one to refuse hospitality, I accepted and sat down. It was the first time I sat at the kitchen table in MeMaw's house. But it wouldn't be the last, not by a long shot.

There were many more visits to that table over the years. Nan served the first meal she ever cooked for me at that table. It was there that she first showed off the shiny new engagement ring that I had scrimped and saved for. It was there that we all held hands while we said grace over each meal. We sat around that table to eat fresh-still-warm-from-the-oven oatmeal cookies that our daughters baked with careful oversight from MeMaw. I sat at that table with a cup of coffee, and asked PawPaw if I could marry his youngest daughter. That table is where we brought our brand-new daughters, tiny and perfect, to be oohed-and-aahed over by their doting grandparents.

And the feasts it has seen! At various times it held bar-b-que from Dreamland, the smoky goodness teasing us and filling our noses long before the first bite. And speaking of bar-b-que - remember those Ribs from PawPaw's grill, dripping with his special sauce? Fish freshly caught from the Gulf of Mexico, battered in cornmeal, fried and served up hot and crisp on plates with crunchy hushpuppies and creamy coleslaw. And MeMaw's famous green beans (my favorite by far), with meat loaf and mashed potatoes and biscuits slathered in butter.

When the hurricanes came and took away the power, the grill went into overdrive and neighbors joined us as we sat in the dark warm air around that table, eating steaks and pork chops and hamburgers from the rapidly defrosting freezers; we ate until we could hold no more.

There were the times when the awful news of a death in the family was discussed there. Job losses, career changes, new cars, house purchases, good grades (and some not so good) scholarships and college selections, laughs and remembrances - all of these and more, took place around that table.

Over the years we must have opened a thousand gifts there. How many birthdays and holidays and graduations and anniversaries and engagements have been celebrated there? God knows, though this writer does not – but it is enough that we would have certainly lost count by now, had any of us ever set out to keep track of something like that.

Suffice it to say that we did life around that table. Every major event in the life of our family was somehow connected to that old wooden oval table and its 6 chairs. As the family grew, we brought in folding chairs from the card table set that MeMaw kept stashed in the closet. We sandwiched them around the table, and all snuggled in a little closer together to eat. At times along the way there were infant seats and highchairs and booster seats in the mix.

That table was witness to so much laughter and joy. And a few tears. And some quiet times too.

I recall the last time I sat there with MeMaw. We took her newest great-grandson for a visit. She held him and laughed, and we laughed with her. I may have caught the gleam of tears in her eyes once or twice… and I suspect she saw the same in mine. Or maybe it was just a trick of the light.

I'm pretty sure there was coffee and Pollman's cake that day too. It was a wonderful day and I am glad we made the time to go see her.

And we sat around that very table to plan her funeral; it bore mute witness to our grief as we carefully laid photographs chronicling a life well-lived on its surface and slowly turned the pages of a history now come to an end.

And here we are again today. To celebrate another birthday. Of all days, this may be the most special.

Because it's the last.

This is the last birthday that will be celebrated around this scuffed wooden table with its freight of chairs. Today marks the end of an era.

I look around me at the friends and family gathered. I hear their laughter ringing through this old kitchen. I see their smiles and happy faces as we join together in a raggedy off-tune chorus of "Happy Birthday". I look past them and see the rooms beyond. The bedroom, the living room, the kitchen. All of them are empty. A few boxes are stacked here and there waiting movement to their new home, wherever that might be.

You see, no one lives here now. This home safeguarded its family for six decades. It saw the heyday of Brookley Field, and its decline. It saw the closing of the old Hartwell

Field, and the raising of the new Hank Aaron Stadium. It was witness to the birth of the Beatles and the death of Elvis. Its closets held the psychedelic clothes and go-go boots of the '60's and the floral designs of the 2020's, and everything in between.

It began its life with wall-mounted phones and finished it with wall-mounted Wi-Fi routers. It saw the racial tension of the 60's. And the racial tension of the 2020's. It saw the Vietnam war and the Gulf war. It saw Kent State and Nine-Eleven. It saw the death of John F. Kennedy and the birth of the space program.

It once boasted a fine 20' console color TV that weighed in at about 200 pounds, one of the first on the block. Today we packed up a sleek, thin 40" monitor that weighs less than the schoolbooks we carried home from class every day.

It had a good run – over 60 years. It was a good home. It sheltered the friends and family that we love. It left lots of good memories. It was the only home Nan ever knew until she set out on a new life journey with a certain crazy drummer-turned-businessman.

This house – this home – has seen a lot.

But now it is empty.

So today is the last celebration around the table at MeMaw's. In fact, it isn't even our table any longer. It is going to the home of a couple of newlyweds who promised me solemnly that they would take extra special care of it. It is going to become part of their family story, just as it was part of ours.

Moves are tough. Moving on – well that is tougher still. And yet there is no progress without movement. As Dan Fogelberg so eloquently put it – the gain is always tempered by the cost.

And I realize, as I look around, that this is a sacred space. Maybe the most sacred of spaces.

The Move

Walls and cupboards bare,
an empty room.
Unadorned surfaces stare blankly at me.
Happy laughter can be heard no more.

Silence echoes.

A last stroll through our abandoned home,
memories ricochet and crowd one another;
a reflective man on a final roam.

Silence beckons.

No welcoming aroma of cinnamon spice.
No bustle of busy hands-on clattering pans.
A new home made, and here the empty price.

Silence reigns.

DRUMS

His name was Rusty. He lived on Faure Drive and I lived a few blocks over on Cadillac. Trust me, it sounds a lot fancier than it actually was.

Rusty and I were friends. We did the usual kid stuff that 9-year-olds did back then; climbed some trees, built a fort or two in the woods, and rode bikes. We rode our bicycles a lot on the next block over from Rusty's house. That's where Darlene lived. To these couple of 3rd graders, she was all that and a bag of chips. When we finally drifted off to sleep at night, it was Darlene who filled our dreams.

So, we rode back and forth in front of her house, yelling and making as much noise as possible, hoping she would come out to see what all the ruckus was and give us a glimpse of her. Just a tiny look, that's all we asked. One look at Darlene was enough to keep our pre-adolescent hearts beating nice and strong for the rest of the day.

It was all fun and games during that lazy summer of 1966. Back then, we played outside. Period. You only went inside if you cut off a hand or got hit by a semi-truck, and then it was only to get some liquid lightning (Mercurochrome – remember that stuff? It set you on fire and you forget about whatever else was ailing you) and a band-aid.

But one day Rusty invited me into his house. We were after some of his baseball gear. We went back to his room and there nestled in the corner was a 4-piece Ludwig Downbeat drum set done up in Oyster Blue Pearl.

I have never recovered from that moment.

I was thunderstruck. There was something inherently beautiful to me about those drums – the cylinders of wood accented with chrome rims, and those cymbals; circles of brass topped with their shiny bells.

The drums sat there, silent, just waiting for someone to happen along and give them voice.

We never did get around to playing baseball that day. I sat enthralled as Rusty banged out song after song, playing along with the 45's spinning on his tinny little portable turntable with the white plastic tonearm and the 9" speaker.

I watched in amazement as his feet and hands seemed to go in all different directions at the same time. I felt the punch of the bass drum hammer my chest at the same time the rimshots from the snare and the crashes from the cymbals filled my ears.

It was the best music I ever heard.

Well, as you might guess I immediately began to scheme how I could get a drum set of my own. In school, I doodled pictures of drums and turned in many a paper adorned with pencil sketches of a drum set. I was hooked. I was captured. I was... gob-smacked! (I always wanted to use that word in a sentence. You're welcome!)

In the 5th grade I met Bill, another drummer. I spent lots of afternoons at his house listening to him play and admiring the fluid ease with which he handled the kit. I knew he was the real deal because he could play *Wipeout!*

But still no drum set of my own. I was living in a foster home, and the chances of a foster kid in the late 60's getting a drum kit were about the same as seeing Walter Cronkite pedal fake news or Tom Jones wear loose pants. Just didn't happen.

But that didn't stop me from playing air drums or beating on magazines with old drumsticks I had dug up somewhere. I played air-drum concerts for my sister and her friends. I was convinced that one day I would have a real kit of my own and I wanted to be ready.

When I turned 14, I was living in the foster home of a family who seemed rich to me. I mean they had new clothes instead of hand-me-downs, they didn't use food stamps, and they had a membership to the YMCA... that's rich, right? I figured that this was my best chance to finally score a drum set of my own.

So, in the months leading up to Christmas, I was especially good. I did chores. I said "yes sir" and "yes ma'am". I didn't fight too much with my foster brother. I made sure not to leave the lid up.

Things were looking pretty good for a set that Christmas, but somewhere around November I went off the rails. The security guy at Bellas Hess caught me trying to sneak out of the store with a bag of Hershey Kisses I had shoplifted.

Guess what? No drums that year.

Finally, when I was a high school sophomore, the magic happened. We had moved out of foster care and were living with our real Mom and her new husband. It was my stepdad who made my dream happen at last.

By that time, I had nursed my dream for 7 or 8 years – nearly half my life. After all that time it was fulfilled by a man who six months before had never met me.

He bought me my first drum set. It was a mis-matched collection of wooden shells and metal shells. The foot pedal for the kick drum came apart about every other song. There was a single cymbal stand that would not stand upright (I finally duct-taped it to the floor so it wouldn't fall over again). The cymbals were stamped out of some kind of soft metal that bent when I hit them with a stick. The drumheads did not match and a couple of them had tape holding them together.

It was the most beautiful thing I had ever seen.

I immediately began trying to teach myself how to play. I started with simple songs that I had already mastered in the air-drumming arena and then progressed from there. *"Baby Blue"* and *"Day After Day"* (Badfinger) gave way to *"Take It Easy"* and *"Witchy Woman"* (The Eagles) which gave way to *"American Pie"* (Don McLean). Finally, I was able to pull off a decent version of *"25 or 6 to 4"* (Chicago). I was big time. I was bad. I had arrived.

My buddy Rory had taken up bass guitar about the same time, and he would lug his gear to my house. We set our instruments up in the carport, bass player and drummer, and played along with the little stereo with the blown speakers. (They weren't blown when we started, but it didn't take long.) People would pass on the busy street and honk and wave. It was a friendlier time back then.

We were hoping for a few girls to walk by so we could shake our hair and act like we were cool. But that never happened. We did get a wino once, though. He thought we were great.

I began to play at church with the youth choir. That was an amazing occurrence back in the day. It was a Baptist church. Drums weren't found in Baptist churches. The odds were about the same as seeing Lawrence Welk play a tune by the Rolling Stones or hear Spock cuss. Just wasn't done.

But we did it at our Baptist Church. I played on Sunday nights and occasionally on Sunday mornings if there was a real toe-tapper in the lineup. The glares from the old folks gradually gave way to cautious eye contact and eventually to toe-tapping. Life was simple back then. No one knew that the Bible talked about cymbals.

Early in college I met the guys in a little acoustic band called Asaph (named after King David's Chief Musician, a song leader, writer of some of the Psalms, and get this – a percussionist! Really, he was! Don't tell the folks at church though).

Ray, Jerry, Monie and Betts had a really nice thing going with some pretty fancy guitar work and sweet vocal harmonies. I would go over to Ray's house after work to listen to them rehearse. I reeked of old grease (I worked at a fast-food joint called Crispy Chick) and the smell would drive everybody crazy with desire for some fried chicken. I sat in the corner and kept time, tapping on my knees as they ran through their simple repertoire of songs.

I complimented them and dropped a few hints about how drums would make them sound even better and how I just happened to know a guy. They nodded and kept playing, trying to ignore my increasingly obvious hints.

Finally, I wore them down. I agreed to bring fried chicken to rehearsals if they let me join the band. Reluctantly they agreed. Their stomachs ruled their moral compass... sad really.

We began playing small gigs at churches, watermelon festivals, valentine banquets, that sort of thing. We ended up doing much bigger gigs than that, but that is a tale for another day. However, I do want to mention our first "big gig".

There was a small concert promoter that had booked Scott Wesley Brown and asked us to be the opening act. By that time, I had covered all my mismatched drums in this weird green contact paper so they would at least sort of look the same. I had added a couple more cheesy cymbal stands to the set, but overall, it was… well, it was sad. But it was all I could afford. Crispy Chick, remember?

The big night came. We traveled in a van owned by Ray's brother Kevin. All the equipment and all the band packed in that single van. We got to the venue (ok, tiny church), and set up our gear.

Scott Wesley Brown is a big deal. He has recorded over 25 albums and toured in over 50 countries. At the time we opened for him, one of his songs, "*I Wish You Jesus*", was topping the Christian charts. We were all familiar with his music.

He came out to do sound check. As he passed by my drum kit, he sorta' did a double-take. I was so embarrassed. I told him that I was saving to get a new kit as soon as I could.

He looked at me, shrugged, and said, "I don't know why you would want to do that. These look like collector's items to me." And he walked away.

Collector's items indeed.

There was the coolest music store ever back then – Andy's Music. There was a drum kit in the front display window that made my heart beat a little faster. It was a Tama kit, with concert toms covered in a beautiful Platina finish – it looked like brushed chrome. I went by Andy's every chance I got to drool on the kit.

Jim, the owner, and Mike, the guitar-whisperer who worked there, bore my visits with patience and good grace. (I ended up working there too – but again, that is a tale for another day.)

It was Ray's mom who came up with the solution for my drum set dilemma. She offered to sign for me to finance new drums. I was finally going to get my dream kit! At last!

The interest rate was something like 1,000% or something (anybody remember the 80's?) but I didn't care. I would have gladly paid for the rest of my life for the privilege of owning that kit. (I would of course order a new one. The display model on the floor at Andy's had drool marks on it.)

I will always be grateful to Ray's mom for her support. Not only did she sign for me (and I never missed a single payment, by the way), she let the band practice in her living room until we got so big that we didn't fit any more.

And speaking of big, the Tama kit was sweet while it lasted. But a friend of mine had a set of Yamaha Recording Customs that he traded in. I sold my Tama set and bought his kit. I still have them and have taken very good care of them Bryan!

So back to my story. When I was around nine years old, God put a call on my life to be a drummer.

I am as certain of that as I have ever been of anything. He planted a dream in my heart to play drums and percussion with a band, to travel and make records. And then He proceeded to put people and events in my life to bring every single dream to pass. He is good, isn't He?

I still have my kit. It's not a mishmash of drum shells. It is one of the finest kits ever made. It is a 13-piece Yamaha Custom Recording kit with a set of high-pitch Octobans, a bazillion cymbals, gongs, cowbells, vibra-slaps, congas, bongos, dumbeks, a cajon, Chinese drums, wind chimes, a robo-disc, a bell tree, wood blocks, electronic drums… oh, and a triangle. Mustn't forget the triangle.

I still play. I've never been as talented as some of my heroes like Steve Gadd or Neil Peart, but I've been supremely blessed. When I play, it opens the door to worship in a way that isn't like anything else I have ever experienced. It is a pure worship, the simple delight of playing to an audience of One.

And I have a simple prayer when I am worshipping.

Father, thanks for drums.

BETTS

It was a little thing really. An old newspaper clipping that a friend posted on Facebook. It was an announcement for an upcoming concert which showed the place, the date and time and a picture of the band who was scheduled to play.

But the band wasn't just any band. It was the group that I played with. For a lot of years. We wrote music together, did the arrangements, played the concerts, loaded the equipment, ate at greasy roadside diners, stayed at seedy motels, did a record or two… and laughed. A lot.

But back to that clipping. The photo shows five fresh-faced kids, with nary a wrinkle or a grey hair to be found. The clothes and the hair give away the age of the image, but the faces don't. They are unlined, they are carefree, they are the faces of five folks who are in love with each other.

The photographer caught one of the guys in the band at just the right moment. The rest of us had expressions that ranged from a slight smile to more serious looks (we were a band after all!).

But not this guy. The camera lens caught him squinting a bit against the sun. He was thin, as were all of us. Age hadn't yet had the chance to diminish our dreams or expand our waistlines. He wore an open-necked shirt with short sleeves. And he was wearing a full-on grin.

His name was Betts. Technically that was his last name, but we had two Jerrys, so he just became Betts. We didn't talk about it, or vote on it. It was an organic thing, it just happened naturally. To us he was Betts, plain and simple. He was my friend. He was my bandmate. He was my brother.

When I saw the clipping, it all came rushing back. The years and years of playing together, the crazy antics and miles driven and setups and breakdowns. The amazing experiences, the music, the friendships so close that they endure to this day, some 40-odd years later.

Betts and I were roommates. I was homeless and he found me one night, sleeping in my car. He woke me with a knock on the window and invited me into his small house for "a couple of nights while we sort this out". Those couple of nights turned into a couple of years.

He was the bass player. I was the drummer. Now you have to understand that a drummer without a bass player isn't much good to anyone. We learned that lesson from some of the best in the business.

We were getting ready to record an album. It was to be recorded in a studio in Muscle Shoals, arguably the music capital of the world. Certainly, that little backwater town boasts an incredible group of musicians and an amazing list of hits. The list of Number One records coming out of the studios there goes on and on and on.

That was cool enough but then we found out we would be working with Jerry Masters as our engineer. Yes – THAT Jerry Masters. He did hit records for Paul Simon, Lynyrd Skynyrd, Joe Cocker, Traffic, The Staple Singers, Wilson Pickett, Bob Seger, Cat Stevens, Steve Winwood... well, you get the picture.

Needless to say, we were a bit nervous about recording with this guy. To tell the truth we were afraid that when he heard us play, he would laugh his way into cardiac arrest or something.

With that in mind, we called him up and asked his advice on how we should prepare for our recording project with him. His answer was direct, to the point, and disarmingly simple. He told us to make sure that the drummer and the bass player played the same song.

And fortunately, we did. Betts and I spent a decade or so "playing the same song". We roomed together, played music together, laughed together and grew in the Lord together, although to be completely honest with you, he was always way ahead of me on that front.

He taught me to love good jazz and how to load a trailer so it towed smoothly. From him I learned how to recognize a great bass player. Heck, because of him I know who Stefan Grappelli is!

He taught me about laughter and living in joy. He taught me.

I believe that the music we played helped to draw folks closer to God. And I can't think of anyone else that I would have rather done that with. (Well, maybe Geddy Lee, but he was busy).

So back to the clipping. You see, Betts died last year. He was a young man. He was a Godly man. He was…. Well, he was Betts.

His death left a hole in our hearts. In my heart. And that clipping made it all come rushing back. The years together, the years apart, the years gone by like the arc of a shooting star, beautiful and terrible in its brevity. The music shared, the inside jokes, the puns, the absolute stability of a brother who would do anything, anywhere, at any time for me.

When I saw that old clipping and his fresh face… well, it hit me hard.

I remember the day we did that photo shoot. It was one of those beautiful days that seem unique to the Gulf Coast. The sky was a cloudless blue, with a faint breeze that kept it from being too hot. We were excited to be there, cutting up and goofing off. And clueless of what the future held – good or bad. We were just being present in the moment. I learned that from Betts too.

As I write this, I am listening to The Pat Terry Group, one of Betts' favorite bands. They played one of his favorite songs. It's called "Home Where I Belong". The lyrics are eerily prescient:

They say that heaven's pretty, and living here is too
But if they said that I would have to choose between the two
I'd go home, going home, where I belong

And sometimes when I'm dreaming it comes as no surprise
That if you look and see the homesick feeling in my eyes

I'm going home, going home, where I belong

While I'm here I'll serve him gladly and sing
him all my songs
I'm here, but not for long

And when I'm feeling lonely and when I'm
feeling blue
It's such a joy to know that I am only passing
through
I'm headed home, going home, where I belong

And one day I'll be sleeping when death knocks
on my door
And I'll awake and find that I'm not homesick
anymore
I'll be home, going home
Where I belong

You know, on the day we shot that photo they used in the clipping, Betts didn't know it, but his homecoming was already scheduled. A big party was in the works. Some folks up there were eagerly waiting to see him again. Planners were plannin', decorations and doins' were happening. Food was being prepared. Musicians were tuning up and practicing. A bass guitar sat there at stage left, waiting for its owner to show up. Everything was ready, right down to the sweet iced tea on the tables.

And sure enough one night in early spring, Betts got that knock at his door, just like the song said. Angels escorted him home. He showed up for the party. He's there now. He's not homesick anymore.

And one day, I will see him again. And the bass player and the drummer will play the same song once more.

But this time, it will be for always.

THE SCALE

I've got one of those fancy scales. You know the kind – they don't just weigh you. They get nosy and maybe even a little personal. This thing measures my Protein, Water, Muscle Mass, Fat %, BMI, Nasal Congestion, BMR, ratio of body hair to height, and a bunch of other stuff I can't remember.

It even tells me my body age. I always thought that my body was the same age as I am, but turns out I was wrong. My body age is…. Well, let's just say I'm surprised to still be around!

And this thing talks. Who knew?! A few months ago, I stepped on it and a robotic voice said, "One at a time please!"

Not really, but the number that it displayed for my weight was… terrifying. So, I decided it was time to act. I got serious about dropping some extra weight and as of today I am down around 26 pounds. I have around 11 pounds to go before I reach my first goal, and then will start on Phase II to lose another 20 pounds. Take that, you smart scale!

How have I done this; you might be asking. Well, I am using math. Hang in there, I know when I mentioned math, I lost a bunch of you, but stay with me here, this is good stuff. People pay billions of dollars (that's billions with a B!) to learn the secret of how to lose weight. And here I am about to give it to you for free. Ready?

I spent years researching this topic. I read reams of research while munching on popcorn. I listened to a ton of podcasts while drinking milkshakes. I watched a boatload of videos while sampling various take-out pizza. I talked to experts, doctors, shamans, and one guy that I think may have been an ice cream vendor. He had on a white coat and I mistook him for a doctor.

I plotted graphs and did projections and "what-if" scenarios. I made plans and wrote down SMART goals (remember those? Specific, Measurable, Achievable.... I forget the rest). But anyway, here is the secret. Ready?

Drum roll please. Sorry, although I am a drummer, I can't do a drum roll. Because I'm typing.

Ok, this time for real. Here is the secret to weight loss. Ready? OK! Seven words.

Burn more calories than you take in.

Sorry, I know that seems anti-climactic. But that really is all there is to it. Pretty simple, right?

Well, not exactly.

I had to change my eating habits. Which is to say, eating was a habit. And a bad one, at least the way I was doing it. I had to change my workout habits (OK, you're right, I didn't have any workout habits, so I had to get some). I had to track my weight every day and monitor my calorie intake. I had to eat more veggies and fruits and less ice cream and cookies. It was terrible! It was awful!

It was…. Pretty Awesome. Of course, it took a little time for my body to switch gears and understand what I was doing. At first it thought I was punishing it. But eventually it came around and began to understand that I was actually helping it. I made it learn a new math equation:

Good Food + Exercise = Happy Body

But turns out my stomach is hard-headed. It kept trying to convince me that tortilla chips and ice cream were two of the basic food groups. But slowly my new way of thinking began to sink in and some magic started happening.

So, I'm eating healthier and exercising more. I get a double bang for my buck with the exercise. While I am riding my bike or walking (What's that you say? Do I run? No, never. I had a traumatic experience last time I ran. I stepped in a pothole and my stomach bounced up and smacked me in the face. It gave me a bloody nose and black eye. The wife was convinced I had been mugged. So no, no running.)

But anyway, as I was saying, while I am biking or walking, I listen to praise music, or podcasts, or Scripture, or some really great old CCM stuff (Phil Keaggy anyone?) or some primo jazz. Double the fun!

Now before you get too excited, weight loss is potentially dangerous, you need to know that. The other day I was walking sort of briskly, and my underwear, which by this point are getting a little big for me, sort of slid down. I was around a lot of people and I couldn't figure out a graceful way to fix it, so I just walked funny for a few minutes.

But who cares – I'm losing weight!

I know this post is pretty different than what I usually write about, but it is related. I usually write about my spiritual walk, my family, my relationships, my work, my hobbies, my friends…. well, you get it.

But this journey I am on is about all those things. My health and how I feel affects literally every one of those items. It affects everything I do, everything I feel, everything, period.

But you already knew that didn't you? Some of you healthy folks out there are saying, "What took you so long to figure this out, Newberry?" And some of you who would like to be a little healthier are saying, "Wow, I would like to feel better and be able to enjoy my life more!"

Which brings me to the reason for writing to you. If I can do this, you can do this. We only get one body (I know, I know, mine was big enough to share, but enough about that!). So, let's make sure we take good care of our one body.

Oh, and the other reason I am writing is to tell you to stay away from smart scales – especially the talking ones. Mine irritated me so bad that I.... well, I can't tell you what I did, but let's just say that we are getting a Master Bathroom remodel.

One at a time indeed. I got your "one at a time" right here you bucket of microchips.

Did someone say chips?

BOOKS

Just wow.

I walked through the door and stopped dead in my tracks. My sudden stop caused the guy in line behind me to run into me. I heard him mutter some question about whether my parents were married when I was born, but I was too awestruck to pay him much attention.

The room before me was amazing. It was cavernous. It was huge. It was stupendous. As folks from my hometown in Alabama would say - it was a "big ol' room".

It was breathtaking.

I was standing in the entrance of the library at the Biltmore Estate. It is home to over 22,000 books which line shelves floor to ceiling on two levels. I had never seen so many books in one place.

And these aren't just any books. Many of the books housed in the walls of this chamber are custom-bound in Moroccan leather with gilt lettering and decoration; work done by some of the greatest bookbinders of the time. The fragrance of leather and paper filled the towering space and made it feel cozy in spite of its size. It felt like home.

I wanted to grab a book and sit in one of the sturdy leather reading chairs, adjust the lamp just so, and spend the rest of my life exploring the treasure trove of books-cum-art displayed on the shelves before me.

But when I lifted the velvet rope that separated us common folk from the pristine heaven of leather-bound volumes that lay before me, alarms started alarming, beepers started beeping, and yellers started yelling.

"Hey! You there! Whaddya think you're doing! Get back on this side of the rope!" and before I knew what was happening, I was nearly tackled by an overzealous guard who, quite honestly, didn't look like he did much reading.

I reacted instinctively. My years of martial arts training kicked in (get it? "Kicked in"? Never mind!) and I did a perfectly executed back-spin kick and took the guard out. (Ok, Ok, actually I timidly stepped back to my side of the rope and muttered an apology. Us commoners gotta stick together, right?)

Books. I love 'em. I love to read. Always have. I survived many trials of childhood lost in the adventures of Tom Sawyer or the tales of Jack

London. As long as there was a good book around, I was never too lonely or too scared.

As I read more, my vocabulary grew, which my teachers thought was great. The school bully, not so much. In the 4th grade I single-handedly set a record for the-most-black-eyes-ever-received-in-any-class-anywhere-ever because I was trying out some of the four-dollar words I picked up from my books. Like the time I said something about a thesaurus and the school bully thought I called him a dinosaur.

But I digress.

Books are the bomb. My house is filled with them. Old books, new books, paperbacks, hardbacks, even a few with no covers at all. They fill my great room, shelves in every bedroom, and especially my study. They are neatly stacked by my reading chair and on the table of my porch. Colorful sleeves of newer books vie with the muted tones of old cloth-bound masterpieces. Fancy show-off leather editions flaunt gold lettering and gilt-edged pages. Slipcased volumes show off contrasting covers and spines. Pretty much any size, shape or color can be found somewhere in our little library that masquerades as a home.

And don't be mad at me, but I write in my books. Or most of them, anyway. I take notes as I am reading. I underline. I make comments on the pages and in the back of the book. I highlight. I put those little sticky flags on the pages. I even have a journal that I use to write down key thoughts, neat phrases and cool words. Words like "Intaglio", for example. Cool word.

Oh, and speaking of color, that reminds me. When we moved to Atlanta a few years back, I reached out to a friend of the family who is an interior designer par excellence. I asked if she would lend her talents to helping make our new house a home. She is amazing, and I watched as she and my bride went room to room, converting them from box-filled nightmares to spaces worthy of Southern Living.

But one afternoon when I went to look for a particular book, I made a horrifying discovery. They had arranged my book collection by the color of the covers! And some of the books were turned backward so that the pages were visible but the spine was not. Holy moly, what is the world coming to? The next think you know people will stop listening to vinyl records!

Anyway, they were good sports and helped me reorganize. I hope one day they will forgive me for my poor taste in home décor.

I began collecting books when I was a wee little lad and it is (yet another!) hobby that has grown over the years.

For instance, take the leather-bound edition of Shakespeare with an inscription dated June 22, 1866. (Don't really take it, it was just a figure of speech). Or the set of Dickens that I picked up at a local bookstore for twenty bucks. Seriously, like a 10-volume set for $20. I felt like I should go to confession for highway robbery when I left the shop.

I love signed copies and limited editions. A former boss of mine got me going on the autograph thing. He gave me a copy of "*Apollo 13*" signed by the astronaut Jim Lovell. One of my favorite authors is Pat Conroy. I got a chance to meet him years ago. He signed my copy of "*The Prince of Tides*", and I went on to collect signed copies of all his books, including one I found at the local thrift store for $2.

One of my favorite places to score those increasingly rare autographed books is Alabama Booksmith in Birmingham. Their place is very cool – pretty much every book they have is signed by the author!

And speaking of bookstores - years ago, in my hometown of Mobile there was The Haunted Bookshop, run by Mary Francis Plummer. She was a gray-haired, soft-spoken fount of knowledge. She told me story after story about writers and books and the art of the written word.

The shop was as spooky as the name implied. Books lined sagging shelves. They were stacked on the floor and piled on every available surface. There was a path cleared which wound from the front of the place to the back, with lots of places to get lost. The smell of coffee hung in the air no matter what time of day. A radio somewhere way in the back played old jazz and classical tunes in turn. Just perfect.

As a kid, I spent a good part of my minimum-wage earnings on books carefully selected after hours of searching those mysterious shelves. While my friends were buying sporting goods and betting on the New Orleans Saints, I was buying books. I spent so much time there that Ms. Plummer and I got engaged. That ended badly when her husband found out.

And near my current home in Atlanta is another of my favorites. It is called Underground Books. Why did they name it that? Well, because it is underground. Seriously. It is the coolest little shop you've ever seen. You walk down a few stairs and enter another world. The afternoon light that filters through the windows is that special shade of gold that makes the place look magical and peaceful. It's how I imagine the light looks from the reading lamp next to the good Lord's easy chair.

There are shelves and shelves of books neatly arranged by topic and author. Notecards with recommendations and Staff picks are tacked here and there. They have a display case for some of the more rare and expensive volumes, and I always stand there a few minutes, wishing and daydreaming. The staff has gotten to know me, and now when I come in, they give me a Windex wipe to clean the nose prints off the glass when I'm done.

Speaking of Atlanta, if you are ever in the area, be sure to check out A Cappella Books and Atlanta Vintage Books. I promise you won't be disappointed.

I wouldn't be a real American if I didn't mention Square Books in Oxford Mississippi. On a trip west a couple years back I stopped in for a pleasant afternoon in what their website calls "Four stories on five floors in three buildings one hundred feet apart". Rumor has it that John Grisham sightings are a pretty frequent thing around there. I wasn't fortunate enough to run into him, but I did score a couple of first editions he signed. Then I went across the street and gorged myself silly on southern cuisine at the Ajax Diner. I swear it was like being in one of Grisham's books.

One last thing - I've had the good fortune of having a couple of books published. In one of them, Dean, the main character, finds a first edition Jack London at a rummage sale:

"Dean lifted the book from the ragged box and carefully opened the front cover. The smell of age, dry and evocative, drifted up from the pages and filled Dean's nose with memories; old libraries with the afternoon sun slanting in through tall windows, illuminating dust motes floating in the warm rays; schoolrooms with low shelves filled with books waiting patiently for someone to discover their stories and secrets; thrift stores with their freight of orphaned books hopeful for a new home…"   -
excerpt from "Almost There"

I guess that about says it all. Now if you'll excuse me, I have some underlining to do. I have a good chair, a good lamp, a cup of good coffee and a good book waiting. It's a best-seller. In fact, it is the best-selling book in all of history. Can't wait to see what it has to say.

CHRISTMAS SHOPPING

It was 1972. I had just turned 15 and my sister was 11. We had moved back to live with our real mom a couple of months before and were hoping that our decade-long stint as foster kids was over - for good this time.

We had enrolled in new schools and were well on our way to making new friends. Life with mom was, so far, turning out to be great. She had been a waitress pretty much her entire life and for now was working at a restaurant downtown called Korbet's where the tips were fairly good. So, we had a roof over our heads and food on the table.

We were still kids, but we had some sense of what mom had gone through to get us back. She had been an alcoholic since her teen years but had gotten sober and this time looked like it just might be the charm.

As I became an adult, I realized a little more about the demons she must have faced on that journey to sobriety, but as a kid, I was just happy to be home.

December was fast approaching and with Christmas on its way, my sister and I began to plot and plan for how we might be able to buy mom a gift. I had a part time job at Thom McCann after school and on weekends, fitting shoes for a living. That was one smelly gig, let me tell you.

Platform shoes were the thing that year; 3-inch platform soles and 5-inch heels. Everybody wanted to be Elton John.

Using the money from that job, plus some that I had saved from mowing yards around the neighborhood at our last foster home, we planned to go to town and find mom the perfect gift.

We lived in Prichard, Alabama. It wasn't as rough then as it ultimately became (I rode through there a year or so ago and found myself wishing I had remembered to bring a Sherman tank along), although it was on its way. Back then, it was still safe for a couple of kids to wander around. We lived a mile or two away from downtown, and on a sunny, cold Saturday morning sometime in early December, we set out on our gift-finding mission.

I had checked the cash situation, and it was looking like we might have enough money to buy gifts for mom and a few other folks we had on our list and maybe have enough left over for lunch. I didn't tell my sis about lunch because I wanted to surprise her.

We arrived in town just as the stores were opening. Downtown Prichard was in full holiday dress, with tinseled windows and gaily decorated trees. The lampposts were festooned with tinseled bells and trumpeting angels, with a Christmas stocking sandwiched in here and there.

There was Christmas music playing from speakers fixed to the outside of some of the buildings, each one playing a different song, creating a pleasant jangle of holiday favorites. The air was brisk and scented with hints of peppermint, evergreen pine and hot chocolate.

There was a full-service pharmacy not far from the shoe store where I worked. I had scoped it out in advance, and it looked like an excellent candidate for us to score all our gifts. But to be sure, we investigated a few other businesses. There was a jeweler (too expensive), a clothing store (no clue what clothes mom would like), and a hardware store (hammer, anyone?). We passed the shoe store where I worked just in time to catch a person who was stumbling out the front door, tripping over their brand-new 5-inch heels. How on earth did Elton manage to walk, dance and even play piano with those contraptions on? He must be a real musician!

Finally, we made our way to the Pharmacy. It was lined with Christmas lights all along its front, and Bing Crosby music greeted us while we were still on the sidewalk outside.

We opened the door and Christmas hit us full force. It was one of those old-fashioned drug stores with the soda-fountain counter along one wall, lined with stools. You could sit down there and get the world's best ice cream, sundaes, floats and milkshakes. They had a short order grill with the best fries you ever put in your mouth; hot and dripping grease. The homemade burgers were good enough to slap you nekkid and hide your clothes. I ate many a hamburger from there when I worked downtown. Thankfully this was all before they invented cholesterol.

This place was a Christmas wonderland. There was a toy railroad that ran around the entire store. It ran on a track mounted a few feet from the ceiling. There were Christmas lights and toys and tinsel everywhere; Christmas trees twinkling with lights and dripping with icicles. There was one of those silver trees with the colored wheel that turned it different colors; Red, Green, Yellow, Blue, over and over again.

Sis and I walked the aisles up and down, carefully considering different gift options for mom and the others on our list. Every endcap offered a new temptation. Finally, we made our selection. We got mom a set of glasses that looked perfect for drinking iced tea. I got my friend Rory some cheap cologne (anybody remember BRUT?). We got our stepdad a small tool set, and I got a little bottle of perfume for my girlfriend. (Yes, I had a girlfriend. Yes, I agree with you, the girls must have been desperate. Or kind. Or something.) Anyway, I got her the perfume and she wore it to school, much to my heart's happiness.

When we finished, I still had some coin, so I asked my sister if she wanted to go bowling. There was a bowling alley where my friend Rory worked not far from the drug store. We walked over and rented some shoes.

I paid for three games, thinking that I didn't want to humiliate my little sister too bad, so beating her in three games was just the right balance between making sure she kept adoring me as her amazing big brother but not smacking her confidence around too badly.

Three games later, as I turned in the shoes the guy behind the counter commented that he had never seen a girl whomp a guy so badly in bowling. And a little sister no less. Très embarrassing, dude. Turns out my sister is some kind of a bowling savant or something. My ego still hasn't recovered from the whipping she dealt me in 1972.

But I wanted to show her that I could take my beating like a man, that it was a simple matter of me having an off day, that I was still the king of big brothers. So, I invited her to go with me and my battered confidence to Hot Dog Heaven for lunch.

The name said it all. You walked into the place, and it looked and smelled like every greasy spoon you ever saw; it was like the apotheosis of all greasy spoons throughout history.

There was a jukebox in the corner playing the latest Top 40 hits (no Christmas music in this joint). The floor was black and white checkered tile. The walls were done up in wood paneling gone dark with age and grease. Faded pictures of food hung here and there, no doubt new sometime around 1940 or so. In a few areas, the pictures were missing, leaving lighter-colored squares on the paneling.

There was a plastic menu board that had at some point in its life been a white color, but these days sported more of a faded burnt orange look.

The menu board had those black plastic letters and numbers stuck into grooves spelling out the menu options and prices. Over the years some of the letters had gone missing, so you had to be a bit of a cryptographer if you wanted to place an order. There were Ha b gers, Fr3nch Fr e , Oni0N R1Ngs, and so on.

And there was the menu item we came for, the lunch of champions, the epicurean, the gourmand, the connoisseur's delight, the bon vivant…the Ho Dg.

You could get those babies grilled, fried, broiled, boiled, sautéed or raw. They were available in lengths of 4" (the little sister size), 6" (the normal person size), 12" (the big brother size), or 36" (the puke all over your shoes size).

Anyway, we got our food and made our way to our table, a scratched-up Formica job that wobbled like a deck chair on the Titanic. It was scarred up with hieroglyphic initials and so-and-so luvs so-and-so and the like. Felt like home.

While the Doobies serenaded us from the old juke box in the corner, sis and I laughed and joked and noshed on our Ho D gs like they were the best thing we had ever tasted. And perhaps they were. We were out of foster care. We were young and alive. We had our whole life ahead of us. It was Christmastime.

It was the best Christmas shopping experience of my life, and every year around this time I think about it and vow revenge for my bowling embarrassment. I promise to find another Hot Dog place that rivals Hot Dog Heaven, and a drug store that embodies all the spirit of Christmas and buy gifts for everyone on my list.

But as you have no doubt figured out, those things are gone. Vanished like the 5-inch heels that folks used to buy. Those days are gone never to be recaptured.

But one thing remains.

Still love you sis.

THE ANNIVERSARY

Thirty – eight years.

For four decades – nearly half a century - we have been bound together in that mysterious joining called love, which depending on circumstances has masqueraded as devotion or patience or passion or even exasperation. But always the joining has proved more powerful than anything that sought to erode it.

September 25, 1982. A day that will always burn brightly in my mind. Michael Jackson's "Thriller" is about to rocket to the top of the charts, complete with guest appearances by Vincent Price and Eddie Van Halen. The first CD player has just been sold in Japan. Disney has opened Epcot with its iconic geodesic dome.

Gas is less than a buck a gallon and it cost us $.20 each to mail our wedding invitations. Uncle Sam told AT&T they were too big for their britches and ordered them to break up (turns out the joke was on Uncle Sam, AT&T waited a few years and then consolidated again). The introductory issue of USA Today is published and promptly sells out, and doctors perform the first successful artificial heart implant. Fans get a chance to peek into Elvis' inner sanctum as Graceland opens its doors to them for the first time.

There is trouble brewing on the horizon. Interest rates are creeping up. Time Magazine has named its Man of the Year – and it is a computer. The U.S. has just entered a major recession. Tylenol capsules laced with potassium cyanide have killed 7 people in Chicago.

But we don't care about any of that. We are in love and the world looks rosy and beautiful. We have no money, but we have jobs. We have no savings, but we have dreams. We don't know what the future holds, but we have faith.

We have a 13" black-and-white TV that will pick up 3 stations if we get the tinfoil wrapped just right around the rabbit ears. We have a setup that includes a card table and 4 folding chairs which bravely calls itself a kitchenette (I finally sold some of my drums so we could buy a real dining set). We have a used green-plaid couch and chair that her folks gave us before they went and bought new stuff that wasn't quite so… visually entertaining.

We are playing house in our small apartment that we decorated together. What we lack in style and funds we make up for with creativity. There are books and albums and we have a working turntable. Life is good.

The wedding was…. interesting. We bought some silk flowers and candles, and created arrangements we thought would look perfect in ceramic cups that the bridesmaids would carry down the aisle.

And they did look perfect indeed. Right up to the time the candles caught the flowers on fire. There was a muted scream or two, but they were able to blow the flames out and the procession continued to the alter, trailing smoke like a trail of incense following a priest. Good times.

The ceremony was lovely, although the Unity Candles were stuck and required me to grab them with both hands and get a couple of my buddies to help me pull them out. Oh, and speaking of friends, some wit painted "Help Me" on the bottom of my rented patent leather dress shoes so the crowd got a good chuckle when we knelt to pray.

We left the church amid a shower of rice thrown by our well-wishing friends and family. We got into my 1978 Honda Accord hatchback festooned with "Just Married" messages on all the windows and drove off, trailing tin cans and balloons which some of the guys had strung behind the car. That was a thing back then.

Our honeymoon had a perfect start. We left the church and headed across Mobile Bay to have a post-wedding romantic dinner. We arrived at the restaurant and relaxed in our first few minutes of marital bliss.

We ordered some food, and we sat making small talk. I ran my hand through my hair. I do that sometimes when I'm nervous. As my fingers combed through my hair (still jet-black in those days), little white grub-looking things fell out on to the white cloth tablecloth of the nice restaurant. Tiny pieces of rice.

At first, I was mortified, but that quickly turned to laughter. My bride began to shake little pieces of rice from her hair as the other diners looked on, wondering what on earth was crawling out of our scalps, and why we were laughing like a couple of crazy people.

We arrived in Gatlinburg on a drizzly Sunday evening. The weather wasn't cold enough for a fire, so we jacked the air conditioning in our room down to somewhere between "Popsicle Toes" and "Teeth Chatter" and built our fire anyway. They still had wood-burning fireplaces back then and came around every morning to refill the wood bin.

The next day we took in the sights of the town and the mountains. We visited the shops of real artisans and craftsmen up and down the main street, with nary a T-Shirt shop in sight. Wood carvers, soap makers, leather workers, painters and other artists worked their magic as we watched. We stood transfixed at the big front window of the Rocky Mountain Candy Kitchen as men dressed in all-white created piles of taffy and fudge out of sugar.

We visited The Village and met the organ grinder with his little monkey. Yeah, seriously. A real monkey and a real organ grinder. The monkey immediately fell in love with Nan, so we had to go by twice a day so she could feed him. I noticed that he was beginning to eye me with bad intent, so I broke off the visits.

As we walked around, my bride noticed that people seemed to be looking at us, sort of staring. She asked me about it. In my most matter-of-fact tone of voice, I told her that all newlyweds glowed for the first 48 hours; it was a medical fact proven by good men of science. (This was the first of many exaggerations that she would have to endure for the rest of her life, delivered by a loving husband wearing a dead-pan expression).

She didn't believe me, but a few minutes later a little old couple (probably around the age we are now!) stopped us. "Are you newlyweds?" they asked. "Yes", we replied, "How can you tell?"

"Well, you just glow!" came the reply. Score one for the home team.

We ate dinner at The Peddler, which we couldn't afford, and liked it so much we went back the next night. We ate picnics by rushing streams flowing through the ancient cathedral of the forest. I discovered that the mountains were my soulscape. (Her's is the beach. I know because she reminds me whenever we are overdue for a visit there.)

Our first Christmas was eventful. We searched for the perfect tree. In fact, we went to every tree lot in Mobile, Baldwin County, Pensacola, and the Mississippi Gulf Coast. Dozens of lots – hundreds even. Then we went back to the first place on our list and bought the first tree we looked at.

We took it home and put it up in our brand-new tree stand. We decorated it with new glass ornaments we scrimped and saved for, and bought from Sears. The tree looked beautiful, softly glowing with its wrapping of lights twinkling off the $20 ornaments. It was perfect. For about one minute.

Then it fell, breaking most every one of our hard-bought decorations.

A year or so later we moved into our first real house – it had a back yard and everything. The guys from the band helped us move our few belongings and I remember walking around the empty apartment and feeling nostalgic and grateful for the shelter it gave to our fledgling marriage. And hoping that the building super wouldn't notice the scratches along the wall from my drums.

We brought our first daughter home to that little house with its tiny nursery and bare yard. We transplanted grass runners from Pawpaw's yard so we could grow a lawn. We planted roses and I talked to them because my bride told me if you talked to plants, they grew faster. One day I was engaged in a deep conversation with the rose bush and noticed my next-door neighbor watching me carefully. Never could get them to join us for dinner after that.

We learned our second daughter was on the way and knew we were outgrowing our little home. We picked out the property for our next one. It was in a more up-scale neighborhood, which meant there were no cars up on blocks in the front yards. Never in my wildest dreams did I think we could live there. In fact, several years before, we were out for a Sunday drive and rode slowly through that exact community, admiring the stately brick homes and carefully manicured lawns. I told my bride that the only way we could live in a place like that was if she was a maid and I was a butler. And yet, there we were, picking out a piece of property to build our dream home.

Thirty-eight years.

Thirty-eight years of special Christmases, trees decorated with memories of people and places, and the joyful sound of barking dogs and screaming children; of Barbie cars and dress up dolls and make up mirrors.

Picnics at the park, days at the beach, and building snowmen. Moving trucks and weddings. Funerals and dance recitals, cheerleading and college admissions. Trips to Disney World. Drinking hot chocolate as we waited for Santa to show up at the end of the Christmas parade.

Choir concerts and football games and halftime shows and PTA meetings and graduations. Trips to the emergency room and consults with doctors and taking care of each other. School plays and award ceremonies and band concerts. And grandkids.

Thirty-eight years of doing this thing called life together; life in all its fragile elegance, elliptical and mysterious.

When I vowed me to you, I had no idea what the years ahead would hold. Still don't. But I know someone who knows every minute of every hour of our lives. He is the One who loves us with a fierce and undying love. He is the One that gives every good and perfect gift.

Like the gift of thirty-eight years.

PECANS

It is the fall of 1970. The new Ford Pinto with its fastback shape is all the rage. In a stroke of marketing genius, Ford sold the first Pinto to an elementary school teacher in Pinto, Maryland. The teacher's name? Mr. Pinto, of course. Don't like the Pinto? Well, you can buy the AMC Gremlin for $1800 bucks.

The crew of Apollo 13 are safely back on terra firma after their near miss with extinction. The Concorde has just completed its first supersonic flight so you can have lox and bagels in New York for breakfast and fish n' chips in London for lunch – on the same day. Football fans across the nation are mourning the death of coaching great Vince Lombardi.

DJ's spin the Carpenters and the Jackson 5. Real vinyl, none of that digital stuff. Elvis is going back on the road after an extended hiatus and in my little town of Mobile excitement is high; the tour includes a stop at that new-fangled round auditorium they built downtown.

Oh, and the Beatles broke up.

You can fill up your gas guzzler for 36¢ a gallon. First class postage? Six pennies. The average working Joe is earning around nine grand a year. A new house will set you back 27 Thou. For a buck, you can buy milk for your Fruit Brute. Yeah, that's a thing. Nixon reigns supreme.

Speaking of houses, that brings me to my story about a couple of foster kids. There was a big brother and a little sister, and they were in a new home. Earlier that year the Child Services folks came to get them. They packed their brown paper bags and got in the nondescript car with its government plates and plastic seats, nervously wondering what the new home would be like. Would the people be nice? What kind of chores would they have? Where would they go to school? Where would they sleep? Would there be other kids there? Could his little sister still host her famous poker games?

The Lady from Child Services drove the plain sedan with black wall tires and no hubcaps to a beat-up house on Texas Street. Now, you have to understand that the neighborhood around Texas Street back then wasn't nearly as bad as it would ultimately become – though it was definitely on its way.

He and his sister were in the back seat and got up on their knees to look out the side window.

They didn't have to unbuckle their seat belts. There weren't any. Not sure how any of us survived to get to the 80's.

They pressed their noses to the rear window, straining for a glimpse of their new home. The house was that no-color gray that wood takes on when it hasn't seen the benefit of paint for a few years. The front porch leaned a little to the left and was missing a board or two. The screen door hung slightly askew. The whole house seemed just a little off somehow. Steps led down to a dirt yard festooned with weed patches here and there.

A lady came out of the screen door and down the steps, nimbly skipping over where one of them was missing.

You can imagine their surprise when the lady looked at them. It was their mom.

They began to scream and shout in excitement and grabbed for the door handle. In the melee they spilled their brown paper bags and mismatched clothes went everywhere. They tripped on them as they scrambled out of the car, trailing pants and shirts and underwear as they ran to their mother, dragging clothes through the dirt behind them.

She knelt to hug them as they ran screaming into her open arms. Tears of happiness ran down three faces – four, if you count the Lady from Social Services – as they embraced.

Moms have their own scent, ya know? The little boy breathed deeply as his mom's scent slipped up his nose, a mixture of jasmine sachet and Pall Mall cigarettes, her brand of choice. Sometimes her scent included whiskey or beer, but not today.

And that was part of the reason they were here. Their mom had worked hard and gotten sober. He figured part of the reason she did it was so they could come home, and his sister could start hosting her poker games for the neighborhood.

So, home they were, and it was a magical summer. Long lazy days sitting in the porch swing, riding bikes, playing ball in the yard, walking across the street to the ramshackle corner store to get soft drinks and candy.

Their mom served them coffee she made in a beat-up old percolator, one of those plug-in jobs with the clear bubble on the top so you could see the coffee brewing. Her coffee was strong enough to stand up by itself without a cup, so they learned pretty quick how to doctor it with plenty of sugar and cream.

And the pièce de la résistance? There was a drug store down the street that served ice cream. A couple of times a week they walked down there and came back with scoops of ice cream piled impossibly high on sugar cones. Lemon for him, chocolate for her.

As summer gave way to fall, their thoughts began to turn to Christmas. In fact, they started thinking about Christmas somewhere right around New Year's Day. They were kids, after all. They were talking about what they wanted to get their mom for Christmas. They were proud of her for how hard she had worked to get clean, and for being able to drive that crummy old broken-down 1960 Studebaker Lark every day while at the same time keeping her cussing under control. Or mostly under control.

One day at the grocery store they saw her admiring a Carnival Glass pitcher set. Something about the iridescent blues, roses and greens seemed to captivate her. The set came with the pitcher and six glasses. A bit of beauty to brighten her world, available for only $40.65. Tax Included.

The perfect gift. But where would they get the money to pay for it?

He and his sister bounced ideas off each other. Maybe he could mow grass. (No mower and pretty much no lawns in the neighborhood). Maybe rake leaves. (The neighbors liked the leaves. They helped cover up the dirt). Maybe they could sell something? (Good, except they had nothing to sell).

I know what you're thinking – the poker games, right? Well, I was only kidding about that. His sister didn't really host poker games. At least not back then. Those came later. And she added cigars for sale.

The answer, like most of the best solutions, came purely by accident. They had just come back from their weekly trip to the ice cream shop. He finished his cone and was eyeing his sister's with obvious intent. She glared at him and told him to back off.

But she was a slow eater and he had warned her plenty of times about the Big Brother Law of Uneaten Ice Cream. That law states that if the big brother finishes his ice cream first, the little sister's ice cream is fair game. Them's the rules man. It's a tough old world.

As he approached her with an ice-cream crazed look in his eye, she bent down and grabbed the first thing her little grubby fist found. It was a pecan.

If you aren't from around here, you may not understand about Alabama pecans. They are huge.

They are heavy. They are the perfect weapon in the fist of a little sister protecting her ice cream.

She chunked it at him. It hit him between the eyes (she was clearly familiar with the story of David and Goliath) and then plunked down to the ground. He bent and picked it up. Suddenly an idea dawned.

"Sis, you're a genius!" he yelled. His sister took a step back. She was used to him yelling at her, but the genius part was new. She needed a minute or two to process things. "We can sell pecans!" he continued. She nodded sort of half-heartedly, thinking maybe her perfectly aimed missile had scrambled his brains.

Turns out that the house on Texas Street was built in the middle of a pecan orchard that bordered a large cemetery. There were pecan trees everywhere. He used to curse them when he rode his bike because the trees dropped those hard-shelled nuts all over the place. If you caught one of those babies just right a wreck was sure to follow. And he had the scrapes and bruises to prove it.

"We can pick up pecans and sell them!" he repeated. "That's how we can earn money to buy Mom that pitcher she wants!" She realized what he was saying, and her eyes lit up. "Yes!" She cried. "Great idea!"

They didn't wait. They headed into the house to get some brown paper sacks (man those things were versatile! Collect pecans, cover schoolbooks, and even serve as luggage for erstwhile orphans.) They came back outside and began their harvest. Over the next few days, they loaded up several bags with the nuts they found on the ground.

There was a pecan company a mile or so away from the house. Tanners Pecans. They grabbed the bags of pecans and headed that way. Turns out that pecans are heavy, so they had to stop every few minutes and rest. He was fine, but he wanted to make sure that his little sister didn't get too tired. He could tell she was getting tired because she kept asking him why they were stopping so often.

They finally made it to the store and handed the bags over, one by one. Mr. Tanner weighed each bag in turn, toting up the freight of their labors, and jotting down the numbers on the wall with a stub of pencil pulled from behind his ear. Her big brother watched in nervous anticipation.

He knew exactly how much they needed. He had gone over the numbers time and time again, calculating the tax so he would have the right total. At last, Mr. Tanner did a final tally and then hit a button on the cash register. A bell dinged and the big drawer slid out.

"Here you go, son, $30.47," he said, pulling bills from the drawer and handing them to her brother. The final coin dropped into his palm with a faint 'clink' as Mr. Tanner shut the drawer.

Her brother looked at Mr. Tanner, then looked at the money in his hand. It wasn't enough.

"Are you sure? Is that all?" Her brother's voice sounded small. It may have trembled a little.

"What's wrong?" his little sister asked, hearing something in her brother's voice. "Nothing sis, it's nothing. We just don't have enough to get mom what we wanted to get her. But don't worry, we can find something else she will like," he finished quietly.

"But she doesn't want anything else!" his sister wailed, tears standing in her eyes. "She wants the pitcher and glasses!"

"I know, sis, I know," he replied. "But we don't have enough to buy that."

At this point, Mr. Tanner spoke up. "What seems to be the problem, young man?"

Her brother looked at Mr. Tanner as though sizing him up to see if he could be trusted, and finally began to explain about the gift they wanted to get their mom, and how they had worked many afternoons to get enough pecans to sell so they could buy the pitcher set. But they were short by $10.18.

"But that's ok," he finished, turning to his sister, "We'll figure something out. Let's go."

He tucked the money into the pocket of his jeans and took his sister's hand. They were almost to the door when Mr. Tanner exclaimed, "Well lookee here! What do we have here?"

They turned and saw him holding a white sack with rope handles on the sides. It was filled with pecans. He put it on the scales, pulled the pencil stub from behind his ear and made a note on the wall. He added a number to the figures there, and they heard him talking under his breath. "Add the eight, carry the one.... looks like I owe you... ten dollars and 18 cents!" he said, opening the register drawer.

"But sir," her brother said, "that isn't our bag."

Mr. Tanner looked around, almost comically. "Well, I sure don't see anyone else here!" he exclaimed. "So, these must be yours!" he said, putting the folded dollars in her brother's hand along with the change. Gently closing the boy's fingers over the cash, Mr. Tanner said, "Go buy your mom that gift, young man," nodding in the direction of his little sister.

So, it turned out that they were able to buy their mom the pitcher and glass set after all. It was even on sale that day, so they got a couple of other small items as well.

On Christmas morning their mom opened the gift, clumsily wrapped by two kids enjoying the first Christmas back with their mom. When she saw what was inside, she laughed and clapped her hands. It was a pure laugh of joy - maybe the purest of her troubled life.

The big brother, all grown up now, thinks about that day sometimes on Christmas morning when he is opening gifts with his own family. And sometimes when it is really quiet and he's all alone by the Christmas tree, with just his thoughts and a good fire, he can still hear his mom's gleeful laughter as she pulled the wrapping from that long-ago gift.

And he thinks, thank you Lord for pecans.

THE CAPE

KA-Powie! SMACK! UGH!

So went the soundtrack to one of my favorite shows when I was a kid. I'm talking of course about… Batman!

It was a race to get home from school each day and get a spot in front of the TV at one of my friend's houses. We had to allow enough time to adjust the rabbit ears so that the skin tones weren't too green. Except for the Joker of course. Green was cool for him.

Once those rabbit ears were just right, we settled in for an episode of crime-fighting *par excellence* – nobody could catch the bad guys like Batman and Robin.

I learned a lot from watching those early episodes of Batman. My friends and I were so enamored of the caped crusader that one of the moms in the neighborhood made Batcapes for all of us.

Imagine it – your very own Batcape! I will never forget mine – it was yellow with a black bat stitched to it.

Wearing that thing made me feel 10 feet tall and able to fly. (And one day, it got too real. I jumped off the roof of my buddy's house. Thankfully I didn't break anything. Unfortunately, Darlene, my grade school crush, wasn't around to see it. But Theresa, the 4th grader who lived across the street saw it and man, was she impressed! More on that in a later story perhaps...)

I learned a lot from those heroes of my youth. I went into college reading comic books and Rolling Stone magazine and came out reading The Wall Street Journal. But I never forgot the lessons from my old favorites. They taught me about character, honesty and how to be tough without being a bully.

From Superman I learned that selflessness and integrity are foundational in the life of a leader. From The Hulk, I found that it is best to keep your cool under pressure.

From X-Men I learned there is strength in diversity, and we should celebrate our uniqueness. And from Batman I learned to swear (Holy BatBelt Robin!) without getting into trouble with my teachers at school.

From Jonny Quest I learned that knowledge is power, and learning is cool.

Daredevil taught me that there are no handicaps, only challenges.

Dr. Strange reminded me that there is infinite possibility if you never give up. Spiderman was a living example that when life brought the unexpected, it was important to find out how to use it for the good of others.

In recent years, the Superhero is back in a big way, and has taken on a whole new persona. Spider Man, Superman, Iron Man, The Hulk, even my old favorite Batman have gotten upgrades in their outfits and their "powers". Superheroes are cool again.

I hope that my grandsons find a Superhero that they can learn from. I worry a bit that the cartoon and superheroes of modern time may have lost some of their…well, wholesomeness. Too much focus on violence and not enough focus on justice, integrity and truth.

Our world needs those attributes like never before. Deception, cheating and outright lying seem to be the rule of the day, even among – make that especially among – our nation's leaders. The concepts of personal responsibility and accountability have faded in favor of plausible deniability and spin.

But our nation was not built on plausible deniability or spin. It was built on the bedrock of

Christianity, faith and the belief in a higher power, a higher way and a higher purpose.

It occurs to me as I write this that I have a responsibility to my grandchildren to teach them the old ways. I have a responsibility to pray and intercede for our nation. I have a responsibility to deal with mercy and grace, but also with justice and truth.

Old fashioned words, those. Back all those years ago I never thought much about them. They just were. They were foundational, they were not for sale.

But now it seems everything is up for sale or debate. Everything is subject to the fickle winds of political correctness that blow, first this way and then that.

Absolute truth is seemingly a thing of the past. But never believe that. We can choose to ignore a truth, but that does not diminish the truth. We can choose to shirk responsibility, but that does not remove our accountability. We can choose to hate, but that will never erase love.

These are heavy burdens for our shoulders, but necessary ones. Hang on, I have something that will help.

I have an old Batcape around here somewhere.

LOUISVILLE

July in Alabama. It's the kind of heat southern preachers are thinking about when they preach fire and brimstone from behind plywood pulpits.

There's a car coming down the road, kicking up dust in the dry heat. The couple in the car are almost to their destination. They pass a sign that announces the name of the town to all newcomers.

The sign is built of brick. It is large and fancy, and to tell the truth, it seems a little grandiose for the town which these days is mostly empty buildings with boards nailed over the windows, like wooden cataracts over windowed eyes.

The town has seen better days. It isn't on the way to anywhere, and unless you are going there on purpose – or you are lost – you wouldn't know it's there. You would think it's in the middle of nowhere.

But it isn't nowhere for her. It's the place that her dad grew up. It's where he left from when he went off to war before he even graduated high school. It's where he knelt in the dirt and kissed the ground when he returned. Her mom grew up just down the road apiece. The same road they are driving on right now, in fact.

Her grandmother ran a country store not far from here. She let her granddaughter filch free little cokes from the old timey red-and-white Coca-Cola freezer with the sliding doors on the top. Her cousin nearly died when a log truck unloaded on him just over that hill there.

Her uncle owned a local farm and spent the last seven decades or so coaxing cotton, soybeans and corn from the clay soil. No, this isn't nowhere. This is home.

She remembers back in the day when the town buzzed with commerce. Trips to the little corner grocery with her Granny. Going to dinner at that diner just across the street. It's boarded up now, but back in the day they served the best hamburgers in five counties. There was even a movie theatre in town.

They breast the slight hill before them. Heat mirages dance just above the cracked black asphalt with its faded double yellow line. Grass grows through the cracks in places. That is some tough grass.

They have come here today on a mission.

They turn off the small road onto an even smaller road – a track really – that circles behind the Methodist Church and into the cemetery. I told you this is home, right? It is. It's the final home for her mom and dad. She has come today to tend to the needs of her folks.

Her mom passed last year on the day after Christmas. She was laid to rest next to her husband on a chilly New Year's Eve, surrounded by the bare limbs of nearby trees climbing into the sky, branches twisted like arthritic fingers. Her folks celebrated the New Year together this year for the first time since her dad passed 16 years before.

But today, the winter is long past, and the heat is here. Sweat drips from her face as she arranges the flowers she brought here today. It soaks into the ground where her folks are buried. Sacred ground.

She works diligently. It is important to get this just right.

She mixes the red roses with the white oleanders. She takes them out and starts over. She stops, staring out in the distance for a few minutes. Sweat – or is it tears? runs down her cheeks. Then she bends to her task again.

He asks her if she needs help, but she shakes her head and continues to work. He moves a few feet away, leaving space for her grief. Her delicate hands work the flowers, moving them this way and that, clipping stalks and leaves, pulling and pushing and replacing flowers until the vase is filled with a perfect arrangement.

She places the flowers in front of the stone with her folks' names chiseled in the granite. There are two dates beneath each name, separated by a single, centered dash. Their life. It began on the date to the left of the dash and ended on the date to the right of it. A whole lot of joy and happiness and living and loving took place in between.

I'm grateful for that dash. That dash brought me the graceful lady who is kneeling not far from me, arranging flowers to honor her mom and dad. She is a southern lady through and through, all graceful and lilac-scented on the outside, full of fierce resolve and terrible strength on the inside. If you are part of her family or circle of friends, she will do anything for you. If you hurt her family or friends, God help you.

The task is done. She calls me over and we stand together quietly, each with our own thoughts, each honoring and remembering in our own way.

Sometimes memories of the dead are more important than discourse with the living.

I realize that Memaw and PawPaw aren't gone. They are in heaven, sure, but that's not what I mean. They are still here. They go with us wherever we go. They live on through us and our girls and their kids.

Without words, we turn to go.

But we'll be back.

Rototoms

Andy's Music was a tiny slice of heaven. You should understand that right up front. They had rows and rows of drum sets. They had stacks of cymbals and racks of drumsticks. They had a glass-fronted case filled with all kind of percussion toys – shakers, tambourines, crotales, afuche-cabasas, maracas, wood blocks, cowbells, finger cymbals, bell trees, chimes – they even had a kokoriko.

If you don't know what all that stuff is, don't worry about it. I only share it because I want you to know that Andy's was the real deal. They got it. They understood musicians and their gear.

There was always music playing in the shop. Usually, rock or some great jazz stuff – Lee Ritenour, Larry Carlton, maybe some Miles, and a new band that was just forming who inexplicably called themselves Toto.

I was in there a lot. I should have been studying or working at one of my two jobs. But the lure of Andy's was too strong. I couldn't stay away.

Many mornings, on my way to class I would stop by and stare in the big display windows at the front of the store, hands cupped around my face to better see the treasures displayed. And the biggest treasure of all was a Tama drum set.

Did I say drum set? No, let me clarify. Let me speak clearly. This was stuff of dreams, the monster, the pièce de résistance, the mother of all drum sets. This was the take-your-breath-away-and-make-your-heart-skip-a-beat kit.

It was a Tama 22" double-bass drum set up with a complete rack of concert toms. 6",8", 10", 12", 14", 16", 18". And let us not forget the two floor toms – a 16" and 18". Plus, their ImperialStar 14" x 8" snare. It was finished in Tama's Platina color which looked like brushed chrome. Beautiful.

So, maybe now you understand why this young drummer had to stop by for visitation rights a few mornings each week. I stood at the front window, my car idling behind me in the otherwise vacant parking lot while I dreamed. What must it be like to sit behind a kit like that, to drive a band's groove with that array of drums at your disposal? I had no clue, but I was itching to find out.

I'm sure that Jim, the owner of Andy's, and Mike, the guitar-whisperer who worked there, knew of my visits. No doubt they were inside the store on some of the mornings when I made my pre-class visits. No doubt they patiently cleaned the smudges I left on the storefront glass after those visits.

Every chance I could, I stopped by. I didn't have two pennies to rub together, and they knew that. But it never stopped them from being gracious and tolerating my frequent drop-ins.

Gradually I became bold enough to start adjusting some of the drum set-ups on the display floor of the store. Mike and Jim are musical geniuses, but neither of them are drummers, more's the pity.

So, I would show up around the time the new kits were scheduled to arrive. I'd help unload the truck, unbox the kits, set them up and tune them. (The famous drummer Peter Erskine paid me the highest compliment imaginable. He was there for a clinic once and asked who tuned the drums. With a dry mouth and quivering voice, I told him I did. He said, "Nice! Best tuning job I've run into in awhile." I rode on that compliment for weeks.)

After the clinic that night I had to drive him to Pensacola for his next gig. Me, in the car for 90 minutes with Peter Erskine! We talked about his work with Weather Report, Stan Kenton, Maynard Ferguson and so many others. Heaven, I'm telling you, heaven.

I had joined a band by this time and was embarrassing them pretty much every weekend in gigs throughout the Southeast. Not by my playing (I hope?), but by my pieced-together-patched-together drumkit.

Ray, one of our guitarists, came to rehearsal one day and said his mom had offered to sign for me so I could finance a kit. She was an angel; do you hear me? When I got the news, I made a beeline to Andy's. I already knew the kit I wanted. Of course I did. A Tama Platina finish.

Nothing so grand as that double-bass kit, mind you. But nothing too shabby either. I wound up with a 7-piece kit complete with Zildjian cymbals. I took them home and the first thing I did was polish everything. It was the most satisfying moment of my young musician life.

Thanks for hanging with me this far. All that is good background for the real story. The RotoToms.

All my interaction and hanging out at Andy's, plus a lot of groveling and begging on my part paid off when Jim offered me a part-time job at the store. This was beyond every dream I could imagine! I was already working at Crispy Chick and at Teledyne Continental and going to school full time, but who could resist a job offer like the one Jim laid on me? I accepted on the spot and started that same day. It started a journey that would last for decades; those friendships continue to this day.

I took care of the percussion shop, dusted all the instruments, sold guitars and strings and sound equipment and pretty much anything else I could do. Sometimes in order to make extra money, I cleaned and repaired drums, or polished cymbals for some of the drummers who came by the shop. I also cleaned and tuned any trade-in drums that came through to get them ready for resale.

One day, I walked by the used gear section and there sitting in quiet splendor was a new addition – a set of Remo RotoToms.

You may not know what a RotoTom is. But you can know this. I immediately fell in love with them. I had wanted to add a set of RotoToms to my setup, but money was a problem. I was working three jobs, true, but tuition is expensive. Even back then. So, not much hope for buying new stuff, especially since I was still paying off my kit.

But that didn't stop me from admiring them. I decided that some lucky guy was going to add them to his kit one day, and I wanted him to have the best set of used RotoToms in the business. So, I got to work.

I disassembled the entire set. I cleaned all the hardware with metal cleaner, and polished the chrome with 000 Steel wool until it gleamed. I lubricated all the screws and the stands. I removed the drumheads and put on new Remo Black Dots, the drumhead of choice back in the day. I labored with an eye for detail, determined that this job would be done right.

I worked on them for 3 or 4 days straight. Finally, I finished them and put them back on the showroom floor. They gleamed mellowly in the overhead lights and I must admit, there was the tiniest bit of lust in my heart.

But I had done my part. Some lucky drummer was going to add those beautiful drums to his set and they were as pristine as I could make them.

They sat for sale several days, with me scheming all the while about how I could buy them. Quit school? Sell some blood? Maybe a kidney? Get my little sister to get a job and give me the money? Sell Amway? But none of my schemes seemed to be the right approach.

Every day when I got to work, the first thing I did was to walk back to the Used-Gear section to make sure my treasure was still there. And you know what happened next, don't you… the day came when they were gone.

My heart fell. I felt deflated somehow. Looked like I wouldn't have to sell that kidney after all.

I moped around the store for a day or two, thinking about the lucky guy who was even now wailing away on some sweet RotoToms. But I'm a pretty resilient guy, and eventually I moved on.

It helped that it was nearly Christmas and business was booming. I didn't have a lot of extra time on my hands to be sad, I was too busy. But from time to time, I wondered about the kit that got away.

On Christmas Eve, just as we were getting ready to close the store, Jim said, "Hey Terry, got a second?"

"Sure boss," I replied. He motioned for me to come to his office. When I walked in, Mike was there, and sitting on the floor next to him was a large box, wrapped and bowed.

"Looks like you guys finished your Christmas shopping just in time," I said, looking at the package.

"As a matter of fact, we did," Jim said. "Open it."

"What? For me?", I replied. "Wow, thanks guys! I'm sorry, I didn't get you anything!"

"Just open it," Mike said, nudging it toward me with his foot.

Well, you know what happened next. I tore the paper off and ripped open the box. There, nestled quietly amidst the packing, was the set of RotoToms. They hadn't been sold after all.

Tears sprang in my eyes before I could stop them, and I couldn't speak. After a minute or two when I trusted my voice, I said, "Guys, what did you do?"

"Merry Christmas Terry!" Jim said. "Take those and enjoy them!"

I did just that. I added them to my kit and played them for years. And every time I unpacked my cases and set them up for a gig, I remembered the amazing gift from my friends.

It's true that I never got them a gift that year. But it wouldn't have mattered. Some gifts can never be topped. It's been over four decades and yet the memory of that gift still burns bright in me.

Thanks Jim.

Thanks Mike.

Merry Christmas.

SOULMATES

For all you lovers, past and present -

To my soulmate –

Everyone wants to be known. To feel as though they matter, as though their thoughts and dreams are important.

Deep in our heart of hearts where only the rarest of visits is granted, each of us wants to have the freedom to open ourselves to the intimate scrutiny of another, to have our secrets studied by one we love. We want to unfold the chart of our soul and invite another to navigate the alien geography of its precarious peaks, valleys and hidden vales.

We want to know and be known, love and be loved, understand and be understood. We want to feel special.

We want to be *celebrated.*

That is what you do for me. You make me feel as though I am someone special – and I feel special indeed, because you have bestowed on me the rarest of gifts – your love. Your uniqueness knows no boundaries, your spirit is wild and unruly and beautiful and untamable. To think that I am the recipient of such a treasure never fails to astound me.

You are the confessional to my inmost thoughts, ideas, insights, experiences. It is as though I can be completely transparent. It is odd; instead of worrying what you might think or do, I somehow seem to know. It is almost as if we are part of the same person.

When I see something that captures me, I almost certainly know it will capture you as well. When I am moved, I know you will be moved. When I am thinking of something, I know somewhere deep inside that you are thinking it as well.

I once heard words that haunt me – *we don't choose love, love chooses us*. I believe in the mysticism of love. I don't deserve or understand how you came to belong to me or me to you, but I will never fail to treasure you.

I celebrate you. Tonight. Always.

I love you.

THE FOURTH

The 4th of July was nearly here, you see. I wanted to find the perfect spot to watch the fireworks. It was going to be my daughter Ashlee's first fireworks show and it had to be perfect.

My daughter was small and we didn't want to brave the crowds at all the popular spots. So, we began to brainstorm. Place after place was mentioned, considered, and ultimately discarded. Too far away. Too dangerous. Too unfamiliar. Just Too.

At the time, my bride was working in a high-rise office building. She mentioned it as a possibility for viewing the fireworks and said she would check to see if it would be open on the big day. It turned out that it was in fact going to be open, and we could even access the top floor!

We made plans to go there to watch what we were convinced would be the show of our lives. We even packed a picnic dinner to eat while we watched.

The much-anticipated day finally arrived. We placed ourselves, our picnic and our cat in the car. Just kidding. We didn't have a cat.

But the rest of us headed out. We arrived at the top floor destination and settled in. I knew that Ashlee was at the perfect age for viewing fireworks.

Before long the show began. Somewhere in the distance we could hear patriotic music; tubas and snare drums and piccolos in precise cadence. The firecrackers cracked. The rockets rocketed.

The explosions lit the night in stroboscopic wonder as I carefully watched my little girl's face. The many colors of the sky were painted on her cheeks and reflected in her eyes which were wide open in joy.

We ate our picnic dinner and watched the show. Sure enough, it was the best one yet. As the last rocket illuminated the night sky, we gathered our things and prepared to leave.

I looked at Ashlee and asked what she thought of her first fireworks display. Wonder was still imprinted on her delicate features in the aftermath of the pyrotechnic spectacle. But overlaying the wonder, I saw a faint worry as she looked at the gray trails of smoke still visible in smudges against the dark night sky.

"Well sweetheart, what did you think?" I asked.

"Daddy, they've ruined the sky", she replied.

I smiled and took her tiny hand in mine. "Don't worry beautiful, the sky is ok. By the time we get home it will be all clean," I told her.

"Promise?" she asked.

"Promise," I told her.

When we got home, I got her out of the car to carry her in the house. Sleepily she lifted her tiny head from my shoulder and looked up. The canopy of dark sky over us was punctuated by brilliant stars, like diamonds on inky velvet. And there wasn't a single smudge of smoke to be seen.

"You were right Daddy," she said, closing her eyes and putting her head back on my shoulder.

I thought about her response to the fireworks, and it occurred to me how often I'm like that. Many times, when I am experiencing something amazing, I let worry creep in and tarnish the joy of the experience. That's silly. I need to let go of the worry, secure in my relationship with my heavenly Dad and His love for me.

No matter what the sky looks lie, it isn't ruined. Pretty soon the stars always shine.

THANKS DAD

It was a hot day in July. July 3, 1972 if you're interested. I was out riding my skateboard in the south Alabama heat. Through the heatwaves coming off the pavement, down the street I saw the car turn the corner and my heart fell. It was The Lady from Child Services.

My sister and I had only been in this foster home for a few months, but we were accustomed to moving without much notice. We shuffled from place to place with all our earthly belongings packed in a couple brown paper sacks.

So, it wasn't exactly a surprise to see the plain gray sedan with its black wall tires and government-issued plates coming down the street and to the place we had called home for the past 6 months or so. Time to move again I guessed.

The car pulled into the driveway and The Lady got out. I could tell right away that whatever news she was bringing wasn't good. You develop a sense about stuff like that as a foster kid. By that time, I had been in the care of the State for more than three-quarters of my life.

The Lady asked if we could talk, and we went into the kitchen and sat down. My sister appeared from somewhere in the back of the house, and we all sat around the table. The silence was awkward as we waited to see what would happen next. Mentally we were packing our brown paper sacks.

The silence built, and finally The Lady cleared her throat and said, "I'm sorry to have to tell you this, but your father was killed yesterday."

My mind did a quick double-take. Wait – what? So, we don't have to move again?

Then the words registered. My dad was dead.

I tried to understand how I felt about it, but I guess it didn't hit me. All I felt was numb, with a bizarre out-of-place relief that the brown paper sacks would not be needed, at least not yet.

Turned out my dad got into an argument with a friend. Words became shoves, shoves became fists, and fists became bullets. Dad was shot and bled to death in the middle of South Hallett Street on the outskirts of downtown, in the middle of an Alabama summer.

I was 14.

The Lady asked me if I wanted to go to the funeral. I looked at my sister, who still hadn't comprehended the news that had just been laid in our laps, and said, "No, it would be better for us to remember him the way he was."

That wasn't hard to do. I had maybe a dozen memories of him, and most of them were not things I cared to remember.

I don't recall much more about that day. I think maybe I cried a little. Or maybe a lot. Like I said, I don't remember. But I do remember that I became even more distant, angry and bitter than I already was.

Fast forward 48 years and 6 days. It is now July 8, 2020. I am 62.

I am reading a book about redemption and spiritual growth. There is an entire chapter devoted to relating to God as a Father. I have to be honest; I struggle with that.

Don't get me wrong – I am much better than I used to be. God used the love He gave me for my daughters to soften me and teach me much about a Father's love. I can relate better to how a father loves his children these days, but that part about how to love a father? Still stumps me a bit.

I had any number of "fathers" during the years I was in foster care. Some were good men, some were not. Some were just evil. And to be fair, along the way, God put a couple of excellent examples in my life (thanks Mr. Koger and Mr. Irby!).

But I gotta tell you, it is still hard to relate to God as a loving Father sometimes. It is much easier for me to imagine Him as impatient, short-tempered and angry. That isn't fair to Him, I know, but I am being honest here.

Some of you can relate, you know? I've talked to a lot of people over the years who can't relate to a loving father. A father who drinks? Yeah. A father who hits? Yeah, that too. A father who is missing in action? For sure. But a loving father who wants the best for his children – that is a new one for many.

And that is a problem, as David's book points out. You see, understanding the Fatherhood of God is central to our faith. If we miss that, it is so much harder to embrace the overwhelming love that He has for us.

So that leaves many of us stuck somewhere between longing for a closer relationship with Him and just giving up out of frustration at not being able to relate to Him as a loving Dad.

That's me. Over the years I have ping-ponged between these two extremes, punctuated by those times when the realization of His love overwhelmed me.

But God is good, isn't He? I went to sleep last night thinking about my relationship with Him and how I want it to be closer and closer, but this father image thing keeps getting in the way.

This morning, I was reading in Psalms and came across a verse that reminded me God is a helper to the fatherless.

Now I have read that passage many times and quoted it many more. But this morning, I suddenly understood in a whole new way.

It isn't just that He helps fatherless kids with the necessities like food and clothing. It isn't just that He provides them shelter. It isn't even that he puts good people in their path to watch over them and watch out for them.

No, it goes much deeper than that. He gets it. He understands that our experience with earthly fathers (or the lack of experience with them) affects us. It affects how we relate to Him.

And so that business of being a helper to the fatherless also means that He will help us learn how to relate to Him as a loving and kind Father; a Father who actively seeks to have a relationship with us.

You know, Jesus' disciple John got it. Here's his perspective in 1 John 3:1. *"How great is the love the father has lavished on us that we should be called children of God!"*

How great indeed.

Thanks Dad.

Thanksgiving

Whatever happened to Thanksgiving?

I was talking to a friend the day after Halloween. They were giddy. I asked them - why so happy? The response caught me off guard as they told me, "It's the first day of the Christmas season!"

Poor Thanksgiving. In a world where Christmas decorations show up in stores about the same time Easter decorations are coming down, Thanksgiving doesn't seem to have much of a chance.

Don't get me wrong - Christmas is special. Especially if you're a kid. But back in the day when I was a kid in grade school (that's what we used to call it before everyone started using 4-dollar words like "elementary"), Christmas season began the day after Thanksgiving. That's when everyone hit the stores, spending the loot they had carefully stashed in the sock drawer. Dimes, quarters, nickels – even pennies – and an occasional dollar bill, hoarded like a miser until the day after Thanksgiving.

Later on, folks started calling it Black Friday, which always struck me as an ugly word to kick off the most joyous of seasons.

As kids, we eagerly looked forward to the cooler temps (we lived on the coast, so it rarely got really cold, although there were a couple of memorable times when it snowed, but that's a story for another day). But around Thanksgiving, the temperature would drop enough for our breath to frost the morning air.

On those mornings, if you were smart, you covered your ears. We all wore crewcuts and it was a favorite pastime of the bullies in school to sneak up behind you and thump your ears. It was cold enough to hurt like crazy and your ear looked like an overripe beet until at least lunch time. And it rang like a fire alarm until sometime around dinner.

Thanksgiving came faithfully each year, bringing so much food and so many relatives. It was like the crescendo that opened the season leading up to Santa's big day.

At school, the bulletin boards were covered with orange pumpkins and brown turkeys; Pilgrim hats and leaves of red, gold and yellow.

One of the bulletin boards in the hallway was sure to feature pictures of the Niña, the Pinta and the

Santa Maria with their wind-filled sails plying waves made from blue construction paper.

The ships were manned by cherry-faced pilgrims on their way to America, wearing those bizarre hats and square belt buckles, carrying guns that looked like trumpets.

Each year we heard my favorite story – the tale of Pocahontas and how she saved the life of John Smith. She saved John, and Squanto saved all the rest.

I wonder if the meaning of Thanksgiving was lost on many of the kids in my class. I'm sure our teachers tried to help us understand the true meaning, but I suspect that it mostly fell on deaf ears.

After all, to be truly thankful, it seems to me you must have something to compare your situation to. If all you've ever known is stability, prosperity, peace and plenty, it is not easy to have feelings of true thankfulness as a kid. You mostly just go from day to day living in your "normal".

But there were a few of us who had some experience with lack in our young lives. By the time I was in grade school I already knew what it was like to be homeless, sleeping on a park bench downtown in Bienville Square with a newspaper for my blanket and another for my pillow.

And I knew hunger too, come to think of it. So, I may have fared better than some of my friends with the whole concept of being thankful.

As an adult, I learned that thanksgiving is a key part of being a happy human. Those of us who walk the planet steeped in hurt, bitterness and anger have little room left for gratitude. As someone who has been there, that journey is hard, let me tell you; it is a map with Self as its destination.

So back to my original question. Whatever happened to Thanksgiving? These days seems it gets lost in the shuffle between Halloween and Christmas. Oh, we may get together with our friends or family to eat ourselves silly and watch some football, but if that's where we leave it, we miss the whole point.

You see, the Christmas celebration has its roots in Thanksgiving. We must be ready to receive all the gifts of the season with an open heart of gratitude.

Thankfulness means we must have a different focus, looking beyond our pain and disappointment, present and past.

We need to see our world through eyes of hope, of belief in a better future, with an awareness that no matter how bad things are, there is someone in greater need than we are.

As we focus on others, the seed of gratitude is planted. When we invest in others, that seed breaks open and begins to grow. The fruit of that seed is happiness.

Gratitude is the key to spiritual growth. A heart of thanksgiving is directly tied to a heart of peace. Focusing on the things we are grateful for brings a sense of hope and joy. And ultimately, it opens the door to a deeper walk with God.

Of course, I couldn't verbalize that as a kid, but the concept was there. I knew that things were not as good as I wished for, but they weren't nearly as bad as they could be - or had been, for that matter. And for that I was a happy little kid.

This year Thanksgiving is especially important. We have been on lockdown for the better part of the year, wearing masks that fog our glasses and hide our smiles – and make us feel we have no reason to smile.

We have witnessed acts of violence and hatred that left us reeling and looking for answers, only to find that the answers raised more questions.

We have watched our nation split into two factions, each confident their way was the best way – the only way – to a true America. As Neil Peart so eloquently put it, *Those who know what's best for us must rise and save us from ourselves.*

We have witnessed leaders of the highest offices in the land cheerfully abandon facts, logic and reason, clinging instead to emotion and slinging insults as though there were prizes involved.

At the end of the day, we are left feeling confused, perhaps a little soiled, more than a little frightened, and just plain tired. Worn-out-right-down-to-the-soul kind of tired.

Yes, I would say that we need to bring Thanksgiving back. Bring it back in a big way, say amen.

So here is what I am going to do. Perhaps you might like to join me.

Every day between now and Thanksgiving Day I am going to write down one thing – just one – that I am grateful for. It doesn't have to be a big thing. Everything counts.

For example, I am grateful that my grandson lights up when he sees me and runs to me with arms held up (unless his Nana is around, in which case I rank somewhere between curdled milk and chopped liver).

And I'm thankful for my family. They love me unconditionally. I hope one day to be the man they think I am.

And I am thankful for you, my friends who read my books and offer encouragement for me to keep writing. Thank you. Seriously.

Oops, that's three things! Sorry, it got away from me.

And that's how gratitude works. When you begin to focus on what you're thankful for, the first one may be a little hard. The second one is easier. And pretty soon the thoughts of gratitude are running through your heart like an Alabama running back through an opposing defense.

So whaddya say? Wanna give it a shot? One thing you are grateful for each day, written down somewhere?

You won't be sorry. I promise.

The Blessing

I wonder what day it was?

When was the day you first thought of your wedding? What did your little girl mind's-eye see? When did you have that first dreamy aspiration of meeting your prince, the young man of your dreams, of starting a life with him?

And I wonder – what was I doing that day, that minute? Where was I and what business occupied me during that split second when the seismic shift occurred; when that first seed was planted in your heart? Did I feel the change as it sent its first delicate shoot up through the soil? Did I realize the inevitability of what that seed, once planted, would grow to be? Did I understand the fruit that it would bear, the fruit of a new life and a new name? That it would grow into a garden of happiness in your own home, a home of your own making?

I wonder what day it was?

And your love… when did that first glimpse happen between the two of you, that first tentative glance across a room or a parking lot or a high school football field? When was that first awkward "hello", and what feelings followed that? How many minutes and hours were spent wondering *will he call me today*?

When was the first time he made you laugh?

I wonder, when was the first time he picked you up for that first date? Perhaps a fall evening with that first hint of crispness in the air, scented and colored by a kaleidoscope of leaves tinted red and gold and brown, as summer gave up her fight?

And what about the first time you held hands, perhaps worried about whether your hands were too hot or too cold or too sweaty or too clammy, when suddenly your fingers brushed and the next thing you knew, you were holding hands like it was the most natural thing in the world.

I wonder, when was your first fight, and what started it? What caused you to put your disagreements aside and forgive one another and move forward in grace? When did you first realize that love is not always joyous and carefree, but sometimes appears onstage in other costumes; costumes of tension and bafflement and disagreement, and perhaps at times even feelings of hurt and betrayal?

How did your love grow? Was it all-at-once, like a baptism of affection, or was it a slow accretion of little acts of kindness?

How often did you watch him when he didn't know you were looking? And what were you watching for? Were you looking for spirituality? Gentleness and kindness? Intelligence and strength?

What did you see? Did you see things that moved you and attracted you? Things that taught you and challenged you, maybe comforted you? Things that interested you? When did you first realize that there was more to him than met the eye?

When was the day that being with him started to feel like home?

I wonder, when did God, the Father who loves you more than you can fathom, the one who covered you in His fingerprints and placed His *kaleo* in your spirit; when He first thought, "I think that he would make a perfect mate for her. Hey Gabriel, come here for a second. What do you think about this? What if we made sure that these two run into each other and…?"

Well, you know the rest of *that* story.

I don't know when any of those things happened. But I do know what will happen today.

Today, we will walk a few steps down an aisle, arm-in-arm. I will walk tall and proud, for you are my daughter, the apple of my eye, entrusted to your mom and I by God the Father.

Today we will walk down that aisle, and the longest walk of my life with be contained in those few simple steps. People with stand and heads will turn to look at you, the beauty on my arm. They will wonder at your loveliness and grace, and comment among themselves what a beautiful bride you are, and they will be right, for you are beautiful indeed, inside and out.

Today we will come to the end of that aisle. Standing there will be your soulmate, the young man that you dreamed of for so many years, even before you knew his name or anything about him. I will look into your eyes, kiss you, and then carefully place your hand in his.

Today I will entrust the care of you, my sweet daughter, my most precious gift, to another man. I will carefully put your hand into the hand of this deserving young man, sealing your union with my blessing.

Then I will go to my seat, where, per your instruction, I will do my best to keep my tears in check.

Today you will take on a new last name and all the joy that comes with that; new initials to accompany a new life.

But – you will still be my daughter. For you carry within you the essence of your mother and I; all the gifts of childhood and young adulthood stitched together with our love and care. Life lessons which were gently taught have shaped you and fashioned you into the amazing woman that you are.

You have our blessing as you begin this next part of your life journey. As you travel, always remember who you are, and *whose* you are, for you carry our hearts in your pocket.

Love,
Daddy

THE CAR DOOR

I called her from work. I asked if she would like to go on a date that night. She said yes.

For the rest of the day, I looked forward to the evening and my date. I left the office early and got my car washed so it would be clean and shiny. It wouldn't do for her to get her dress soiled from a dusty fender or dirty car seat. I pulled to the curb at exactly the time that I told her I would pick her up.

I walked to the door, straightening my tie and making sure my suit jacket was buttoned. I rang the bell and her mom answered the door. Behind her, I could see my date.

There she stood, dressed in her favorite outfit. Her mom had done her hair up in pigtails and she looked adorable. When she saw me, she ran, calling my name with her arms raised.

"Yay! Daddy's here! Let's go!"

And go we did. I took her by the hand as we walked down the driveway. I opened the car door for her, and she got it, wiggling to get situated and trying vainly to see over the dash. When she was comfortable, I fastened her seatbelt, went around to my side, and fired up the car. Off we went on our date.

That scenario happened many times when my daughters were young. I'd call, ask them on a date, and pick them up. We'd go to the movies, or Putt-Putt, or McDonalds, or Chucky Cheese.

As they got older, our times together became more sophisticated; coffee houses, bookstores, antiquing, the Ballet, live concerts, shopping at the Mall, whatever. Didn't really matter where we went, what mattered is that we were together.

My goal was simply to spend time with them. I was an ambitious professional, career-minded and driven to succeed. I worked long hours, traveled a lot, and understood the need for balance. I wanted to be sure that the space between my heart and theirs never got too wide. I didn't want them to start calling me "Mr. Father" or something, you know?

But some magical things began to happen on our dates. We had great fun for sure. Sometimes when they were small, on the day after one of our times together I would find a thank you note decorated with stick figures eating burgers or bowling or playing putt-putt. The artwork was accompanied by a message written in the priceless hand-printed font of a child's crayon.

Sometimes I would overhear them talking to a friend or their mom about our date and what fun we had. Sometimes as I tucked them into bed, they would suggest ideas for our next time together.

I found that on our dates, they opened up to me in a way that wasn't like any other time. I would like to think that I have always been close to them and that we had good, open communication as a matter of course. But on our dates, that increased a notch or two.

Turns our there's something special that happens in a little girl's heart when she spends time with her daddy. Innocence grows into awareness, awareness grows into trust, trust grows into conversation and conversation grows into relationship. And it all happened organically, a natural outgrowth of those special times we spent together.

Don't get me wrong. We had our times of crisis and sparks. There were the normal times when we disagreed about an activity they wanted to do or a friend they wanted to hang out with. Sometimes we had terse conversations about respect and manners and doing chores and what it meant to be a responsible person.

Sometimes we had spirited discussions about attitudes and the impact that our mindset had on our life. There were pointed talks about hard work and earning your own way. Both my girls were strong young ladies and our worldviews sometimes collided.

But thankfully, those storms didn't define our relationship. They created a sort of balance as each daughter tested the boundaries set by their mom and I. And the time I spent 1-on-1 with each of them helped ensure that our open conversations continued.

Something else happened as a result of those dates. It caught me completely by surprise. My daughters learned how a boy should treat a girl; how a man should treat a woman.

I realized this truth when one of my daughters had a date with a guy from school. The young man pulled to the curb and honked his horn. First of all, he was late. Big mistake. Promptness is the courtesy of Kings. My girls heard that more than once.

As he honked impatiently, my daughter stood at the door, partially in disbelief, but mostly in that irritation that Southern women seem to have from birth with the men in their lives. You can see it in their eyes.

The guy honked again as she stood at the front door, looking out the window, shaking her head slightly back and forth as in "I can't believe this putz is blowing his horn for me to come out."

Finally, the young man got out of the car and walked to the door. He rang the bell and I answered.

"Hi, I'm here to pick up your daughter for our date," he said. "Is she ready?"

I saved my dad speech because I knew this poor guy was about to get an earful from a young woman whose "Southern" was just now blooming.

About that time, she came in from the other room. She gave him a glance that pretty much smoked his eyebrows off, and they headed down the walkway to the car.

He went around and got in behind the wheel. She went to the passenger side and stood there.

He cranked the car and was about to put it in gear when he realized his date wasn't in there with him. He looked out the window and made a "what's up?" gesture with his hands. She just stood there.

Finally, this poor guy, who still hadn't realized that his date was over before it began, got out of the car, walked around to her side, and opened the door. She got in and off they went.

I never saw him again after that.

I realized as I watched this drama unfold that my little girl had an expectation that her car door should be opened. On every date with me, I opened the door for her. Every time she saw her mom and I go somewhere I opened the car door for her mom. (By the way, I still do, all these years later. Guys, you should try it sometime.)

And the expectations didn't stop with opening a car door. My daughters expected their beau to be kind, considerate and well-mannered. And woe to the guy who failed that test.

I have to say, my girls have dated some pretty impressive guys. One of them dated a young man who was a model for a high-end clothing store. It was a weird experience to go into a dressing room there and see a picture of my daughter's boyfriend posing in his underwear, I gotta tell you. He was a smart, good-looking kid who drove a nice car, but he didn't make the cut.

Another kid was the proverbial "most popular guy in school". I noticed that he wasn't coming around much anymore, so I asked her about it. Turned out that he was disrespectful to one of the teachers in class one day and used some foul language. My daughter ditched him like a rented mule.

They don't play, I'm telling you.

Well, both my beautiful girls eventually found the man of their dreams. And I must tell you, they did good.

Both of my sons-in-law are top drawer kind of guys. Each of them asked permission to marry my daughters, and they passed the Dad's-Questions-To-Make-You-Uncomfortable Test with flying colors. They are intelligent, respectful, diligent, thoughtful, hard workers and ambitious. They get along with each other and with the family as a whole. Our family time is generally filled with sweet fellowship, good conversation and laughter. Oh, and food.

And after all these years, I still call and ask my daughters on dates. Although these days I have to ask their husbands' permission first.

And you know what? I still open the car door for them.

I hope my sons-in-law are paying attention.

THE DANCE

I need to let you in on a secret. I was not supposed to dance.

When I was coming up, the adults leading my Baptist youth group discouraged dancing. When we asked them why, they told us that if we started dancing, we would wind up necking in the woods. Honestly, that thought had never crossed our minds, but the more we thought about it, the better it sounded.

So, we skipped the dancing and went straight to the woods.

But we kept the beat alive. We organized clandestine parties in homes where we gathered, carefully checking our backtrail and arriving in discrete groups of two or three so as not to draw attention.

We posted lookouts, clean-cut kids who stood out front with a Bible, to throw off any suspicion. I'll tell you the truth, never was there a speakeasy during Prohibition that was as carefully guarded as the locations of our youth dance parties.

We brought our favorite records – 45's mostly. You could stack those babies on the turntable, and they would play one after the other, dropping on the platter to ensure an uninterrupted flow of tunes. Some of the group favorites were the slow songs.

Put on *"Precious and Few"* and dim the lights, and Presto! you had a room filled with couples dancing awkwardly, trying to slow dance without getting too close to one another. We might have been rebels, but we still listened to our mamas.

I was the main DJ for those gatherings. I brought my collection of 45's in a box, each record in a plastic sleeve, in alphabetical order. (Don't judge. When someone calls for the Allman Brothers, you don't wanna have to dig through 200 singles to find it.) But sometimes, I brought out the big guns.

Make that The Big Gun.

The Best of Bread. Not a single – no sir. This was a full-length LP. 12 songs of magic, 6 to a side. The album of choice for young adolescent males hoping that a slow dance might result in a kiss. Or maybe two.

It was Side One that held the magic. 17 minutes and 10 seconds of slow dance heaven. Here's the secret. The six songs on the first side were all slow songs. Every. Single. One. You could drop the needle on that baby and were assured of at least a song or two before the girl you asked to dance got tired and dumped you for one of the other guys in the youth group.

But we learned that our chances for that elusive kiss increased with every song. So, we played the percentages. Song 1 (*Make It With You*) was 3 minutes and 15 seconds of warm up. Somewhere during song 2 (*Everything I Own*), if things went according to plan, she would put her head on your shoulder. And by song 3 (*Diary*) – it was time to move in for the kiss.

If it hadn't happened by then, odds were pretty good that you were outta luck.

But sometimes we would strike pay dirt, the motherlode, the unicorn of dance parties; the full-side dance. Yep, she would dance the entire first side of the album with you - just you. Song 4 (*Baby I'm-a Want You*), song 5 (*It Don't Matter to Me* – but trust me, it mattered, it mattered a lot), and song 6 ("*If*" – and by the way, if there was ever the perfect song to end an album side, that was it).

If your girl stayed with you for the full side, you were pretty much guaranteed a kiss. Plus, the enmity of every other guy at the party.

As I left my teens, the dancing continued, but now the stakes were bigger.

There was my wedding dance, for instance. No, check that. No dances at the wedding. The youth group leaders were still there, still watching.

But there was the time my boss insisted I attend a Mardi Gras Ball, which in my hometown of Mobile was a big deal. Everyone who was anyone was there. You had to dress to the nines. I rented a full-on tux, complete with patent leather shoes, studs and a real bow tie. I was like, "Newberry.... Terry Newberry".

I'm pretty sure my bride borrowed the actual dress that Cinderella wore to the Castle on the night of the big dance and I gotta say, she put Cinderella to shame.

We rented a limo to take us to the venue and when we arrived, we were greeted by the music of a live band. It was torture for me. My bride wanted me to dance with her. I just wanted to watch the drummer.

Around midnight, I'd had enough. I loosened my tie and took off my jacket, and in doing so, violated every known Mardi Gras Ball protocol. One of the members of the Mobile Mystics (the organization that sponsored the dance - they are called Societies) approached me. He had been on a Mardi Gras float earlier that night and was still in costume.

He had also apparently been in his cups. Deeply in his cups.

He walked – make that staggered – up to where my bride and I were standing calmly, not bothering a soul. "Hey buddy," he drooled. "This here's a respectable place and you gotta put 'cher tie back on, 'n button your shirt collar. You gotta put 'cher coat back on," he continued, falling forward.

I caught him and stood him up. "Dude," I said (sorry, this was a long time ago, so "Dude" was a perfectly acceptable form of address), "I am dressed in a tux. You are dressed like a chicken. I am sober. You are smashed. Go bother somebody else!"

He staggered off and the rest of the evening was uneventful except for when my boss got carried away during one of the more up-tempo dance numbers.

He slid on his knees across the "dance floor" which was pieces of varnished plywood laid end-to-end. Unfortunately for him, there was a place where the pieces didn't exactly line up. He slid across a spot where there was a gap of about an inch or so. He ripped his rental trousers and pretty much ripped his kneecap off.

Back on the home front, life continued – the kids came along and there were the dances with my tiny beautiful daughters.

I would put on some records and invite them to dance. We would whirl around the kitchen or living room, with them standing on my feet as we spun and pretended we were dancing at their wedding.

And all too soon, that day arrived. Actually, two days - one for each daughter.

The wedding reception buzzed in excitement as the guests waited for the bride and groom to arrive from the post-wedding photo shoot.

Finally, they made their grand entrance, the bride ethereal and beautiful in her lace-and-beaded wedding gown, face flushed with the excitement of the ceremony and the relief that it was over. I stood watching from across the room, in awe of her.

And then it was time.

I walked across the room, my heart a storm of emotion as I carefully cataloged every sight, every smell, every sound and every emotion. I engraved them on my heart so that I would always remember this day, this experience.

I took her hand for our dance, possibly the most special dance of our lives. Every eye in the place was on the beautiful young woman dancing with me. She was radiant.

We talked of simple things and I asked her if she wanted to dance on top of my feet like we used to. I told her how proud of her I was, and how much joy she brought into my life. Maybe I made her laugh a time or two.

All the while the film reel of my heart was playing reruns of a younger dad with his little girl dancing on his feet.

Later that evening I would dance with my bride, my partner in all the craziness of this life. For years we have danced the dances of love, of sadness, of worry, of lack and of plenty. We've learned the steps of fear and laughter and joy and faith. And tonight, we danced another dance – the ritual dance of giving our daughter away.

My bride never looked so beautiful, so radiant. Someone captured a photo of it, and I have it in my study so I can see it every day. Her forehead is against my cheek, her eyes are closed, and she is smiling.

I love that smile.

Yes, my life has been filled with dances. Too many to count, really. But I'm not done.

Gotta teach my grandkids to dance.

The Den

Ok, Ok, Ok…

Before you start, hear me out.

I know I go overboard at Christmas. It is well documented. Newspaper stories have been written. TV specials have aired. My kids fuss at me about it. Heck, the White House even called one time and asked if I was trying to upstage them. It is a character flaw.

It all started a long time ago.

When I was a kid, like many of you, we didn't get much at Christmas, and usually what we received were used items; donations from some well-meaning charity. But that was cool, I appreciated the thought.

I had no idea what I was missing until That Day.

That Day. That fateful day.

I was 14. It was Christmastime and I was hanging out with one of my brothers from the foster home where I was living. We went to his girlfriend's house. Her name was Beth.

She invited us in and took us to the den, and WHAM! It hit me like I'd been kicked in the head by a reindeer or smacked by the Abominable. The den in her home was *amazing*.

There was a fire blazing in the hearth, bathing the room in a warm yellow flicker. It provided a crackling soundtrack to the experience as the logs sizzled and popped, sending showers of sparks up the flue. The mantle was festooned with evergreen garland decorated with small ornaments and holly berries, all intertwined with tiny twinkling lights.

I'm here to tell you, the room was decorated to the nines. Lights, tinsel, garland, the whole works. Santa Clauses and reindeer and snowflakes and angels and you-name-it. There was even a Grinch.

Every surface was decorated. Every wall had Christmas art. Every table had Christmas figurines. There were Christmas rugs on the floor.

And down at the far end of the room, in the place of honor, right by the front window for the whole world to see, was the tree. Exactly where it should be.

It was probably a 6-footer, but to me it looked 50 feet tall. It filled my eyes and my mind and my heart. The fragrance filled my nose with a scent that to this day I associate with Christmas; bright and piney and crisp and fresh.

The tree was perfectly decorated and surrounded by more gifts than I ever imagined could be found in one place. They filled the space under the tree and around the tree. They were stacked on the furniture. They were stacked on the floor.

They leaned against the walls of the room. They were stacked on the mantle. They were piled next to the couch and the chairs and the ottoman. They were *everywhere*.

There were large gifts and small gifts, square ones, round ones and rectangular ones. There were boxes and bags and ribbons and bows and wrapping in bright Christmas colors. It was a child's Christmas paradise.

Right then and there I made a decision. It wasn't even a conscious choice – it just happened. I decided that one day, I was going to have a Christmas like that. A tree like that. Decorations like that. And gifts like that. Gifts everywhere, all over the place. Not used gifts – new stuff. New stuff for everyone I knew.

And so, it began.

True to my promise, every Christmas I go just a little crazy. I try to find the perfect gifts, and wrap them in brightly colored paper with matching ribbon, and sometimes add a little decoration, like a drum or a bell. And I have a blast doing it.

There is a workstation set up in our home with dozens of paper choices, a ton of ribbons and bows, gift bags and tissue… it's like we hijacked a Hallmark truck around here.

I put on some Christmas music and I wrap gifts while I listen to everyone from Bing to Casting Crowns. I imagine the look on the faces of my friends and family when they open their gift. I hope to give them, for one brief moment, the joy that I felt that day at Beth's house. Because once they feel that, Christmas comes alive.

Now before my Baptist friends get all up in arms and start calling me to tell me about the real meaning of Christmas, I get it. I know that presents and gifts and bows are not what it is about. Christmas is when we celebrate the birth of Jesus. I understand.

Because of that, I try to celebrate my faith every day. When Christmas comes around it allows us all to share the joy that is in our hearts. As Charles Dickens put it so well. *"I have always thought of Christmas as a good time; a kind, forgiving, charitable time; when men and women seem by one consent to open their shut-up hearts freely…."*

That's how I feel. My faith births the joy that began that Christmas in Bethlehem so long ago, and which is cherished and celebrated in my stubborn heart every day of the year. But then Christmas Day comes around and that joy spills over and becomes a splendid madness with giving at its center.

So, I hope that you, gentle reader, you, my dear kids, (and the White House) will forgive me for my indulgences during the season. I promise I am going to be more responsible and not give so many gifts.

Starting next year.

THE FAIR

When I was a kid, October was the bomb. It was the pinnacle, the apex, the month-to-end-all-months. It was the nirvana of the seasons, eclipsing even Christmas, if you can believe that.

How can that be, you ask? Well, it's simple. October brought the Fab Four. No, not THAT Fab Four. My Fab Four included the Fall festival at Morningside Elementary School where I faithfully attended, the chubby kid with the ragged clothes and rosy cheeks and the crewcut. It brought my birthday, which was usually good for some cake and ice cream. It brought Halloween, which meant that my buddy Dea and I would roam the neighborhood in homemade costumes to see who could score the most candy.

And it meant the Fair was coming. Not just any Fair. The Greater Gulf State Fair.

The Fair. Even now the words give me the tingles. The Fair was the event that propped up my childhood. From November to somewhere around February, I was sustained by the memories of my trip to the fairgrounds. Sometime around the Ides of March, I began to look forward to what the coming October would bring.

Looking back, I have to tell you, there weren't a lot of perks to being a welfare kid in those primitive days of the foster program. We didn't have all the great organizations that exist today. There weren't TV commercials that made you burst into tears and immediately pick up the phone to adopt the latest homeless kid. There were no movies starring Mark Wahlburg about the cool factor of foster care. There were no online resources geared toward helping folks be better foster parents.

I'm very glad that we have these organizations and programs now, but it wasn't a thing back in the day.

No, in those days, foster care existed as a shadowy subset of society. You didn't talk about being a foster kid. You avoided attention. When kids at school asked why your "parents" looked so old, or why your school clothes were so raggedy, you suddenly turned into the Class Clown and diverted their attention elsewhere.

But there was one perk that nearly made up for all the lacks.

On the last Saturday of October, the Fair was in town. On that day, foster kids got to go for free. Yep, you heard right. Free. Free admission, free rides, free shows, even free Fair food.

Each year, that wonderful Saturday morning would dawn bright and crisp. There would be a hint of fall in the air. (OK, so by 11:00 a.m. it was as hot and muggy as ever. After all, folks, it was Mobile Alabama. But hey, you take your tiny joys where you can find them.)

The Welfare Lady would show up in that nondescript 4-door Chevy or Ford that screamed government-issue, and off you would go. From 9 am to 1 pm, you were as free as that fabled bird Lynyrd Skynyrd sang about. Four hours of unbridled fun. Four hours to roam the sawdust paths of the fairground and be a normal kid.

In those days, the fairground was at Hartwell Field, the old baseball stadium in Mobile. It was built in 1927 and featured all the latest in baseball field amenities, including parking for 1,000 cars. On opening day, nearly 10,000 fans crowded in to watch their favorite sport. Babe Ruth and Lou Gehrig played there. Mobile boasted being the birthplace of the likes of Hank Aaron and Sachel Paige. Baseball fever ran high in the city.

When interest in baseball began to wane, they needed different revenue streams, so they opened the stadium to host agricultural events, rodeos, traveling circuses, and the Gulf State Fair.

The Fair began in 1955. The early days featured a few juggling acts and a fresh-faced singer named Elvis Presley from over in Mississippi somewhere. Elvis liked playing there so much that after his first gig, he wanted a contract so he could come back for the next four years. He asked for $1,600, $400 per year. Seemed like a "fair" price at the time. Did you see what I did there? "Fair" price? Never mind!

But riding in the back of that plain gray sedan chauffeured by the Welfare Lady, I didn't care about any of that. I just wanted to get to the fairgrounds, jump out of the car and get lost for a few hours in the wonderland that was the Greater Gulf State Fair.

It started with the smells. You remember the smells, don't you? When you opened the car door the smells hit you like a soft pillow to the face. They enveloped you. Fried corndogs, popcorn, and sizzling onions, caramelized and hot off the grill. Candied apples. Cotton candy. Roasted peanuts. As you walked on the sawdust through the Midway past each ride, the smells came at you in waves.

You knew it was a mistake you would regret, but invariably you would grab a corndog in one hand and a cotton candy in the other hand and scarf it down. Then go back for seconds, making sure to slather plenty of ketchup and mustard on the corndog, and not get any on the cotton candy. Now you were ready for business. Time to do some serious exploring.

As you entered the Midway, the sound assaulted you. It came from every direction. Hawker's calling out from the Guess-Your-Weight booth and the Ring Toss game. The thump of deep bass coming from the 18" speakers surrounding the rides, each playing a different song. The screams of kids as the rides rocked them and shook them and took their breath (and in some unfortunate cases, took their lunch). The mechanical noises were all around you – whooshes and squeaks and beeps and bells and the clashing metal of the rides.

And speaking of the rides. I remember the rides, their names seething with musicality and strangeness. The men operating seemed to be a dangerous breed, a contentious tribe.

The Tilt-a-Whirl with its combination of spinning cars and up-n-down herky-jerky motion. Talking about losing your lunch – the danger of this ride was if you lost your lunch, you might well encounter it again as the car was spinning.

Then there was The Zipper, which was like some madman's demented version of the Ferris Wheel.

There was The Flying Bobs with glittering cars that spun round-n-round while they careened up and down on a circular platform that went faster and faster. The ride operator, usually a drifter that up until that week had been sleeping under the bleachers of the stadium, kept yelling, "DO YOU WANNA GO FASTER??!" and all the brain-damaged foster kids yelled back, "YESSSSSSS!!!!"

The Crazy House with its spinning corridors and mirrored halls. The Haunted House with its quick entrance into the dark and surprise appearances of witches and monsters alive and bloody with dayglo paint.

Sideshows, like the one where a real man gets shot from a real cannon. The Flying Dutchman Pirate Ship which swung back and forth until you were sure you were going to fall out and take a few of your friends with you.

We had The Rocket. The Helter Skelter. The Fireball. The Hurricane. The Monster. The Rainbow. The RoundUp. The Wipeout (this was one of my favorites because about every other song they played was… well, Wipeout).

The Ferris Wheel was there and from the top it seemed you could see almost the whole city. And you dreamed that one day you would have a girlfriend and you would take her to the fair. At sunset you would ride the Ferris Wheel. And when you and your girl were at the very top, the wheel would stop and rock slightly in the cool dusk and you would kiss her.

Hey, don't judge. I was nine.

And then there was the DOUBLE Ferris Wheel, maybe the most iconic ride of the fair. It was not for the faint of heart when it did its big loop and the bottom wheel became the top wheel.

Down the way a bit were the Bumper Cars, where you could learn what it was like to drive in Atlanta traffic. The Merry Go Round which was pretty much for sissies. You had The Teacups and The Scrambler.

Yep, there were any number of rides ready to help an overzealous kid lose the corndog-and-cotton-candy-souffle he had gobbled down so innocently only a few minutes before.

Way back at the extreme edge of the Midway were the freak shows. (Please forgive me, I know that is politically insensitive, but that is what 9-year-old boys called them back in the day.) Most of these were closed to kids but we managed to sneak in to see a few. (If you were careful, you could wiggle under the edge of the tent where it wasn't pegged down too tightly.)

We looked in wide-eyed wonder at The Bearded Lady. The Siamese Twins with two heads and one body. The Headless Woman (who talked to the crowd from her still-alive head, held in her lap). The Wolf Boy. The Four-legged man. The Lobster Boy who only had two fingers on each hand. The Armless Woman who drew a picture with the pencil held between her toes while we watched in breathless amazement.

Thankfully we are more sensitive and civilized these days and we don't have shows like that anymore. Plus, we don't need them. We have Wal-Mart.

But back to the Fair. Let us not forget the music. Every booth, every ride, every food wagon had its own music blaring. It was a delicious cacophony of sound. The Beach Boys singing about those *Good Vibrations. Sunshine of Your Love* by Cream. *Wipeout* by the Surfaris. *House of the Rising Sun.* Hendrix with *Watchtower.* The Jackson Five, the

Beatles, The Temptations, The Byrds, The Doors. Hit after hit after hit.

And the *pièce de résistance*? You guessed it. That old anthem of defiance. *Born to Be Wild* by Steppenwolf. That record was like the Theme Song of the Universe the year it came out. It was playing *everywhere*. Still is, come to think about it.

The music experience at the Fair only got better. There were live bands playing. Local acts mostly, but they had real drummers.

I would push my way to the front of the crowd in front of the stage and watch the drummer with the shiny cymbals and the drums done up in red or blue sparkle, or maybe in that cool pearl look just like Ringo's drums. (In later years, the kits became more extreme, with clear shells and multi-tom set ups, but those early days were all about backbeat and innocence.)

I stood there, eyes glued to the middle of the stage, watching every move. For a few minutes I was lost in the rhythm, the pure emotion of the music.

In my little-boy mind's eye, I was up there on the stage, playing that kit, driving the band. (In an interesting turn of events, years later I played with a band at the Alabama State Fair. As we played that day, I looked out from the stage across the audience, and flashed back to all those years ago, to the psalms of that lost season. I noticed one little kid in the crowd watching me intently, and thought to myself, one day kid, one day. Never stop dreaming.)

For a few hours on those crisp October Saturday mornings, I wasn't a foster kid. I was just a regular kid out enjoying the day with a lot of friends. For a few hours I was the king of the world, storing up memories that would be my refuge for the weeks and months to come.

Over the years, the faces have faded, the songs have changed, and the Fair has evolved. It is much more civilized these days. It is buttoned down and smooth shaven. You won't find a freak show anywhere and the food vendor booths have been replaced by food trucks that display Health Department scores.

The fairground is no longer a hastily thrown together affair; they have their own power grid and health care facilities now. They even have their own Security, a thing unheard of (and unnecessary) back in my day. They have slick marketing and corporate sponsors. The days of hiring hobos to operate the rides are long gone.

But the past is never far away. It hovers over the Midway like the-ghost-of-carnivals-past. You can catch glimpses of it from the corner of your eye between the tents and the food trucks and the whirling rides.

It walks on stealthy cat feet, careful not to intrude but always watchful. It lives on in the smells and sounds and sights of the Midway.

I don't know if foster kids still get to go to the Fair for free. I don't even know if they would be interested, what with this being the age of video games and iPhones and TikTok.

But I hope so.

Because it's October.

A Father's Heart

The heart of a father is a complex thing. It is made up of gruffness and prickly cheeks, of strong arms and butterfly kisses.

It is made up of strong hands, rough and callused, which are nonetheless able to somehow mend the tiniest of broken toys and give the gentlest of caresses. It is made up of good smells; of sweat and cologne and sawdust and coffee.

It is made up of too many hours spent working to provide "stuff" to a family who would gladly forgo some of the baubles and bangles in exchange for more time with dad.

The heart of a father is strong and sure on the outside, but on the inside rests the real truth of things. Sometimes anxious, sometimes caught in the misfire of regret, sometimes weepy, it is at odds with the smooth granite façade he tries to present to sons and daughters.

The heart of a father is a room filled with pictures of little league games and dance recitals and backyard cookouts. Of trips to the lake, of building sand castles on the beach and of going into the deep part of the ocean where only daddies can go, with children on his shoulders holding fistfuls of hair, and filling the air with joyful screams.

There are movie reels in this room of birthday parties and prom dates and graduations and teaching eager teens how to drive a stick.

It is a room of books filled with letters thought of but never written, of words planned but never spoken, of trips plotted but yet to take.

It is a place of mended disagreements and summer walks and time spent praying outside closed bedroom doors, standing sentinel over innocence. It is a place of mumbled prayers and second guesses and spraying kids with the water hose while washing the car.

It is a quilt work of joy and hurt and love and worry. It is patched together with a hundred "I-love-you's" and a thousand "I-wish-I-had-done-that-differently's".

It is money secretly tucked into pockets and purses and wallets, magically to be found when the need seems greatest. It is checking the oil and filling the fuel tank and cleaning the windshield before the daughter heads back to the university.

The heart of a father is a lovely place, cluttered with the tools of love and patience and kindness.

The heart of a father is a mystical place, filled with the magic of dads that somehow appears at just the right time.

The heart of a father is a place filled with unmatched pride and feelings too powerful to be expressed with the frailty of words. It is a place of an earthly father learning how much God loves him through the love he has for his children.

It is a place where long nights are spent in prayer. It is a place filled with the best of wishes, the darkest of worries, the brightest of hopes and the most powerful of loves.

The heart of a father is a sacred place.

THE NOTE

It's a brand-new year. A brand-new page in the notebook. A blank Word document. A brand new, clean slate.

This year hadn't gotten very far before it went sideways. Maybe we were all expecting that a little bit; the thought that there was more trouble brewing maybe got packaged in our hearts along with the hope for a better year.

It's easy to be discouraged. Goodness knows there have been plenty of reasons to be anxious, worried and concerned. It is all a bit overwhelming, to tell the truth.

You know, maybe some of us want to give up a little; maybe hibernate until all the bad blows over. Maybe keep our heads down and hope for the best. But there may be a problem with that.

See, we need each other. That is how we were created. This past year has been a full-on assault on our togetherness.

I was watching a concert video recently and found myself nostalgic over crowds. Yeah, crowds. The gathering of lots and lots of folks in a contained space sharing an experience – a concert, a ball game, a play, a movie…seems like a long time since we did those things.

Like I said, we need each other.

So, what can you and I do to send some small positive energy out into the madness that is our current world? What can one person do against such overwhelming anger and noise?

We can encourage one another. Yeah. That's it. Encouragement.

A few years ago, I managed the BellSouth Mobility Customer Operations team in Birmingham. I had over a hundred people on my team, and it was a little tough to get to know everyone.

On Monday mornings, I got to the office early and ran all the stats and metrics from the week before. I highlighted the top performers of the week. Then I wrote a notecard to each of them thanking them for their great work and telling them how much I valued them and how important they were to our team.

Each Monday morning, I walked around the office before anyone else arrived and left those cards on their keyboards so they would be sure to see them when they sat at their desk. I did that every week.

After a year or two I was promoted to the network team and moved on from my role in customer ops. It was a tough move; we had grown together as a team and I forged some wonderful relationships.

One day, I was selected for jury duty, and went downtown to do my civic good deed. As I sat with several hundred others in the waiting area, waiting for my name to be called, a woman approached me. She called me by name.

I looked up and she asked, "Do you remember me?"

I did. She was a member of that customer ops team I managed several years before. She was one of our online reps. I said, "Of course! How are you?"

"I am doing well," she said. "I thought that was you! I came over here to show you something."

From her purse she pulled a piece of paper that had been folded and refolded so many times it was threadbare. It was held together in places by tape.

Unfolding it carefully, she held it out for me to see. I recognized my own handwriting. It was one of the thank you notes I had written her for doing a great job.

She said, "I have a team of my own now. I think of you often, and I carry this note with me to remind me to always care for my team the way you cared for us."

I was speechless. The note was over ten years old.

That one note, that small act of kindness which probably took me a couple of minutes to write, had set in motion a chain of influence that I could never have imagined.

So, what can we do?

We can encourage one another. We can say kind things and do kind things. We can be helpful. We can choose to not participate in the hatred and fear and ugliness of the world around us. We can share a little light.

People matter. All people. I have a friend who is a bit of an introvert. At the top of the whiteboard in his office he wrote a message to himself. "It's about the people."

It is about the people. The current political climate will come and go. Businesses will come and go. Technology comes and goes. But people are the center of it all. They are the innovators, the inventors, the literal lifeblood that makes the whole world work.

We are each unique. We are each very different from each other.

And we are all the same.

We all have dreams. And hopes. We all worry about our friends and our families. Our loved ones occupy center stage in our hearts – that is true for all of us. We each have someone we love and something about which we are passionate. Each of us has tremendous gifts and talents.

And all of us have the capacity for fear. And for worry.

So, let's share one another's burden. Let's lighten the load with a helpful hand, a kind word, a smile. Let's do a good deed, write a note of appreciation.

Let's listen to one another and take the time to care for each other. Every investment in another human being, no matter how small is powerful and sets off ripples that would amaze us if we could see the ultimate impact of each of us have on others.

Let's love one another.

Because you never know who you might run into at jury duty.

THE TEACHER

She had a gift. From early on, animals and children were drawn to her. Not kidding here.

When she was a baby her mom and dad would put her in a stroller for a walk around the block and the neighborhood dogs would line up and follow them. They would carefully approach the stroller and gently sniff her hand and then offer their heads for a pat or two.

Same with kids. As she grew, other kids just seemed to be attracted to her. When her little sister came along, she became the perfect playmate (until she became a teenager, but that is a tale for another day).

Her mom was the director of a child care center, and often would take her to work. She interacted with the other kids at the center, especially the little ones. They sensed her special gift and responded to her.

It was obvious to her parents that God had placed a special calling on her life to teach. She was gentle and patient with others. She had experienced adversity, and this birthed in her a compassion for kids and their struggles.

So, it was no surprise when she came home from school one day and announced that she wanted to be an elementary school teacher. And further, she wanted to work with inner city kids.

Mom and dad were elated with the news of her decision to become a teacher. Maybe not so much about the inner-city kids... after all, they lived, well…in the inner city.

But her mind was made up. She went off to university. Her dad cried and moped around like it was the end of the world. In a way, it was. His little girl was away at school. She would return one day, he knew that.

But he also knew that she wouldn't be the same little girl who left. There would be a young woman returning in her place.

She studied, worked incredibly hard, made new friends and began to thrive. Her grades reflected the hours spent in darkened study halls. She was driven by her passion – her calling – to teach little ones.

Dad and mom visited often and were amazed at this young lady who showed them around campus.

They could see the ghost of their little girl in the face of the young woman she had become.

She was articulate, well-reasoned, and funny. And beautiful. And driven. Her passion for teaching had only gotten stronger.

The years went by, and the big day finally arrived. They proudly watched her walk across a lighted stage to receive a hard-earned diploma. Big steps across a stage in front of thousands of people. Impressive. But the next steps she took proved to be even bigger.

She landed a job and began her teaching career with a thorough cleaning of her new classroom. Next came decorations, wall art and learning tools in colorful shapes and sizes.

They hung from the ceiling. They graced the walls. They covered the cabinets and she even put them in strategic places on the floor. Oh, did I mention that she funded all of this – every red cent – out of her own pocket? That is passion.

She began the daunting process of teaching young minds how to learn, how to think, how to reason.

She developed relationships with the kids, and they learned that she loved them. She met with the parents and they learned that she could be trusted.

She met with the school Administration and they learned that she was more than competent.

She was compassionate, focused and driven by a love for her kids and a calling to her craft that defied all obstacles.

When a tornado came through the small town where she was teaching, she was among the first teachers on the scene. Her dad warned her that many of the roads were still impassible, there was a lot of damage and it was dangerous. Her response was simplicity itself. "My kids need me."

So, she braved the danger and went to her kids. When they saw her, they ran and embraced her. Some of them cried. Some of them were in stunned silence. Some of them stared off into the distance, vacant-eyed and confused.

She comforted each one in turn, and then helped them pick from the supplies that she brought and that other volunteers had provided. Water, blankets, food, clothing – items to bring some comfort and normalcy back into little lives that had been shaken by this disastrous force of nature.

And she did it all with a smile. Until she got home.

She arrived home that night with clothes so dirty they had to be thrown away. She went straight to her room and got cleaned up. And stayed there.

Eventually her dad climbed the stairs and softly knocked on the door. "Come in," she said, her voice soft and somehow hollow.

He sat on the bed beside her. She put her head on his shoulder and then the storm came. Tears ran down her cheeks and her shoulders shook with the force of her grief. "Why dad, why did this have to happen? Some of my kids lost their homes. Where will they live? Where will they sleep tonight? I have to help them!"

The world would do well to have more people like her, people who love others and feel their pain.

"Shhh, sweetheart, they are going to be ok," her dad answered, hoping that his words were true. "They are going to come through this and will look back on all of it as a big adventure."

"And another thing," he continued. "They will never – never – forget that you were there today, and what you did for them. Sometimes a simple act of kindness grows into a life-altering thing. That is what you did today, sweetheart. You changed their lives."

Eventually things did return to something like normal, and the school year came to an end. She began the terrible wait that all non-tenured teachers face; the wait for The Call. Will they call me back for next year, or will I be laid off?

The school system was having financial trouble, so it was anyone's guess what the outcome would be. It turns out those kinds of decisions are determined, not by the teacher's results in the classroom, but instead by red ink on some accountant's spreadsheet somewhere.

Well, sometime in late summer she got the call. No jobs right now they said. Maybe next year they said. Sorry, they said.

Her mom and dad drove to the school and helped her pack her classroom. It seemed that each piece of art, each piece of decoration triggered a memory.

Here was the picture Billy drew. He was the quiet one, remember? He never interacted with the other kids, until he drew this picture, and everyone told him how much they loved it.

And this one? Rebecca made it for me. Look, it says "You are the best teacher I ever had." Wow, dad, look at that.

On and on, they packed papers and supplies and cabinets. She smiled a lot. She cried some. She realized that she would probably never see most of the kids again, and that realization brought fresh tears.

But the gift of teaching was still strong within her; her passion for kids was a powerful motivation. She still had the call on her life.

She sent out resumes, driving from school to school to hand deliver them. They showcased her impressive credentials and incredible talents and accomplishments.

But no job offers came. The red ink, remember?

Her dad and mom asked the folks in their Sunday school class to pray for a new teaching job. Weeks went by – nothing. More weeks – still nothing. It began to look as though she would not be teaching that year.

One Sunday, one of the ladies in the Sunday school class stood up and made an announcement. She said that during her prayer time, God told her that on Monday, the next day, a job offer would come.

Now, I know what you are thinking. God told her that? Sure, and I have some oceanfront property in Arizona to sell you. But guess what? The next day the call came, right on time, just as promised.

The call was for an opening in Hattiesburg Mississippi. It was an inner-city school. Would she come for an interview?

She would. She went the very next day to talk with the principal. The school was in the middle of low-income housing.

There were kids in the street who watched her as she drove by. They were dirty, playing in yards where weeds grew up around junked cars and broken-down refrigerators. The weed-choked yards surrounded patched-together shacks with cardboard covering missing windowpanes like some crazy checkerboard.

She told the principal of her desire to teach inner city kids and shared a bit of her education and working experience with him. They offered her the job on the spot. Classes began in less than two weeks. Could she be ready?

Yes, she could. Her clothes were packed in record time. A U-Haul was rented. Dishes and furniture were purchased for her new apartment. Everyone in the family, plus a few friends, helped with the move.

The first day of class arrived along with a group of students that were poorly clothed, poorly educated, and poorly acquainted with discipline.

A few days into class, one of the kids – a six-year-old – urinated on her as she sat at her desk. Another day, one of the kids – another six-year-old – threatened to kill her. And showed up the next day with a box cutter fitted with a new blade.

But she made friends with some of the other teachers and set about the task of doing what she was called to do. She was a teacher. So, she taught.

As the year progressed things became increasingly difficult. Students were unruly. They were disruptive. They were dangerous.

And the parents – well, some of them were worse. It seemed that many of them viewed school as pretty much as a source of free meals and baby-sitting. Helping their kids with homework? Fuggit-about-it.

And the principal of the school was…. well, let's be kind and call him clueless. It was his first time in a role of this sort, and he was learning. Slowly. Like at glacier speed.

She continued to teach. She made care packages for the kids to take home. Clothes, toys, and even food so that the kids would have something to eat on the weekends. She gave them gifts for their birthdays and at Christmas. She was a teacher. So, she taught. And loved.

She made many tearful calls home. She told her mom and dad about the kids and their homelife. She called them by name. She wept over them.

But she was confused. Why were things going so wrong? Why had God brought her to this place only to be threatened and intimidated by the kids, the parents and even the school administration? If God brought her here, why was it so hard? What good could possibly come from this?

Her dad tried to assure her that everything would work out, because all things work for good, right? But even he was getting a little impatient. Many times, her mom had to stop her dad from hopping in the car to pay the principal a visit. A personal visit, a visit to help encourage the principal. Strongly encourage, if you get my meaning.

Many prayers were prayed. Why God? Why is this happening? What is the purpose of all this? But God remained silent on the subject.

Until one day, God turned to Gabriel and said, "Hey Gabe, watch this!"

Gabe watched as all the questions about "why" were answered.

That answer came in the form of a tall lanky Sergeant. U.S. Army, thank you very much. He was stationed near Hattiesburg. He met a beautiful southern girl at church. She was a teacher. She was from Alabama. The deep South. He was from Chicago. The North.

He could barely understand a word she said, but he liked the way she said them. She thought he talked funny with his "you guys" and such. It was a match made in heaven.

And the rest, as they say, is history. They started dating and they fell in love. They got engaged, they got married. He was resplendent in his dress blues, medals pinned to his chest. She wore a lacy wedding dress just like the one she had been dreaming about since she was five. They got a house and a dog and lived happily ever after.

So, I guess God really did tell the lady in the Sunday School class that there was a job waiting. It turns out that He actually does talk to us. Who knew?

It also seems that all things really do work for our good. Because He loves us. And because He wants the best for us. Even when it is hard for us to see it or understand it.

But her students saw it. They understood it. She was the best teacher they ever had.

To this day, they still talk about her. And years from now, when they can't remember their first job or what they had for breakfast, when they can't remember the names of their bosses or even some of their grandkids, they will still remember her name.

They will say it with reverence, with secrecy. They will recite it in praise. They will speak it as benediction, as a blessing. They will whisper it as a prayer; whispered words of thanksgiving and grace. They will sing her name as a canticle of love.

Because sometimes a life transcends a lifetime.

Because she was a teacher.

THE MACHINE

Dean thought back to his first bike. It had been awesome – a 3-speed with a gold metal-flake paint job, a tiger-striped banana seat with a chrome sissy bar, and chopped forks. It even had Crazy Wheels (*lime green*) and was the envy of every kid in the neighborhood.

Dean loved the stares he got as he rode slowly up and down the streets of his small town. As a kid, it was the bicycle of his dreams, but even now, all these years later, he wasn't sure how it came to be his.

Dean's parents were alcoholics. When he was 6 years old, he and his sister were taken from them and placed in foster care. On rare occasions, they would be allowed to visit their real parents. Usually, these visits were done at the county welfare office under the careful supervision of their case worker. But sometimes they were allowed to go offsite with one of their parents for a short visit.

It was during one of these rare offsite visits that Dean's dad asked him what he wanted for Christmas. Dean was around 8 or 9 years old at the time and knew exactly what he wanted. He had been dreaming about it for months. It was a new bike. But not just any bike. It was the baddest bike he had ever seen, the most *dude-I-have-arrived-and-I-*

have-the-coolest-machine-on-the-planet kind of bike. In fact, in his mind he had begun to think of it as The Machine.

He began telling his dad about The Machine, but somehow words didn't seem to do it justice. He couldn't adequately describe how he felt when he looked at it, how it made his heart beat a little faster, and how he daydreamed about riding it slowly down the street with everyone watching him (*especially Darlene, the prettiest girl in the third grade, who he knew would love him if only she got to know him a little better. Actually, a good start would be for her to know his name ... but all things in good time*).

As he talked, looking at his dad, he could tell that his words weren't doing the trick. And then he had an idea.

Not far from McDonald's, where they had gone for a burger and a shake, there was a Western Auto. And that particular Western Auto had a special treasure. It was home to The Machine. Dean knew it was there because he often walked from his foster home to the store just to see it.

"Dad, I have an idea. I can show it to you!" Dean said. "It's in the Western Auto not far from here. Can we go by there on our way back to the welfare office?"

His dad looked at him, blue eyes twinkling. He put his hand on Dean's shoulder. Dean wondered sometimes how his dad's hands, so hurtful when he was drinking, could be so gentle when he was sober. His dad said, "Sure thing, son. Let's go have us a look."

They arrived at the store and Dean was out of the car before it had even come to a full stop. "Come on Dad, hurry!" he said, pulling his dad by the hand. "Just wait, you'll see. It is the coolest bike ever!"

Dean ran to the back of the store where the bike sat in quiet splendor. He knew it was just waiting for him to take it to its new home.

His dad listened as Dean pointed out all the best points about The Machine and why it was the perfect Christmas gift. He was so excited that a few minutes went by before he realized that his dad wasn't saying anything.

Dean happened to glance down and saw drops of water, like raindrops, splatter into the dust covering the top of his dad's work boots. His first crazy thought was *is there a leak in here?* But when he looked up at his dad's beard-stubbled face, he saw the tracks of tears which carved furrows down his cheeks. They gleamed in the light of the showroom.

"Dad, are you ok?" Dean asked, alarmed. "What's wrong?"

"Oh, it's nothing son," his dad replied, his voice cracking. "I'm just glad to see you and see how excited you are about the bike."

Dean nodded, still looking at him with uncertainty. Then he saw his dad hang the price tag, which he had been holding in his hand, back on the handlebars. Dean suddenly understood.

He remembered that his dad hadn't been able to find much work lately. He was living in a boarding house, getting by on food stamps and the occasional odd job.

"Dad, it's OK, I really didn't want this bike, I just thought it had a cool paintjob," Dean mumbled. "Don't worry about it," he continued in a subdued voice. "I wouldn't know what to do with a bike like that – heck, I'd probably wreck it the first day," he rambled on, trying desperately to ease the pain he saw in his father's face.

"Shhh son, it's alright," his dad replied. "Don't worry about me, it's just this pollen. It has me all leaky."

Dean smiled although his heart was breaking with the weight of his father's lie.

The ride back to the welfare office was always quiet as both father and son began to prepare themselves for being separated again. But this day's ride was especially quiet, tinged with a melancholy that made Dean sad in a way he couldn't quite understand.

He went back to school, back to his normal routine. Although his mind knew the bike could never be his, his heart and dreams wouldn't cooperate. His mind kept wandering back to how it would feel to pedal The Machine down the street, shifting smoothly through its three gears, wind blowing through his crewcut.

He imagined riding by Darlene's house. She was the girl of his dreams. In those dreams, she would be in the front yard practicing cheerleader routines. She would call out, "Hey Dean, can I have a ride?" and he would nonchalantly say "guess so" as she climbed onto the tiger-striped seat behind him. She would put her arms around his middle and he would fly up and down the streets, pedaling for all he was worth, master of women and machines, the envy of every 3rd grade boy in the world.

And so, he couldn't quite bring himself to stay away from the Western Auto. He spent so much time there that the manager finally chased him away, telling him to quit wasting their time and to come back when he had some money.

Even that didn't stop Dean from going back to the store. But he didn't go inside. Instead, he stayed outside, pressing his face against the plate glass that made up the front wall of the store. By standing near the middle of the glass and cupping his hands around his face, he could just make out the sleek skeletal silhouette of The Machine sitting in the back of the showroom, kicked over on its kickstand, chrome wheels and gold metal-flake paint glinting in the light, surrounded by lawnmowers and edgers and chainsaws and lesser bikes.

One day, the manager caught him outside the front window lost in a daydream. He stormed out the front door, screaming at Dean to beat it, go away, scram, get lost. Startled, Dean tripped and fell on the front walk, tearing his jeans and skinning his knees and the palms of both hands. He got up running as the manager, a fat, middle-aged man who was going bald early, ran after him down the sidewalk yelling at the top of his lungs.

The manager chased him for nearly a block before he stopped and bent over with his hands on his knees. He was gasping for breath. Dean slowed to a trot, and then cautiously circled around, facing his pursuer. He took a couple of steps back toward the man, who was still breathing heavily. Dean could hear the harsh rasp of each breath. It sounded like a bellowing train.

Sweat tattooed his dress shirt, which had come untucked from his pants. His black tie was loosely knotted and hung down the front of his shirt like a dead eel.

Standing up, he looked at Dean as he began to tuck his shirt into his slacks, working around an impressive beer belly. It looked like the man had swallowed a basketball.

He was still breathing hard. "Kid, I told you to stay away from here!" *Breath.* "I am tired of cleaning your snotty nose and greasy handprints off the glass." *Breath.* "If I catch you here again, I will give you something you won't soon forget!" *Big breath.*

Dean looked back at the sweaty overweight manager. His oily hair was hanging in his eyes as he removed his glasses and began to furiously polish the sweat off them with his tie.

Dean stood there, warily watching the man, not saying anything.

"Didn't you hear me!? I said scram!" the man screamed at Dean, spittle flying from his lips in a thin foam baptism. "Get outta here before I make you wish you had never seen me, you little useless piece of trash!"

Dean walked a couple of steps closer to the man, keeping eye contact, but careful to remain out of reach. It was a lesson he had learned from dealing with his drunken father.

"Kid, are you listening? I am warning you. You better move!"

Dean had been quiet up until that point, but the man's last statement broke through his silence.

"I heard you. Tell me fatso – can you hear this?" Dean's small voice rose in fury as he picked up a rock from the ground. Winding up like a big-league pitcher, he let the rock fly.

At any other time, in any other universe, the rock would have sailed harmlessly past the man, skipping benignly across the vacant lot behind him. But not today. Today, the rock left Dean's fist like a rocket on a mission, straight and true. It flew in a perfectly flat trajectory and hit the erstwhile bully square in the nose.

The manager of the Western Auto screamed in agony and sat down suddenly as though he was held together by a number of springs that all gave way at the same time. Dean clearly heard the loud *click* of his teeth coming together, biting off a piece of his tongue as his backside hit the pavement, hard. Another scream. He clasped his hands over his face as blood from his ruined nose and bleeding tongue seeped through his fingers.

"That's what you get for trying to bully a little kid!" Dean screamed at the man.

He never went back to the store after that. As Christmas approached, he dutifully acted excited about the upcoming Christmas morning, although he knew what he would find under the tree.

Well-meaning people contributed gifts so that foster kids like himself would have a Christmas. Which was cool. Which he appreciated. The problem was the *kind* of gifts they gave. They were mostly used and broken.

Dean remembered the presents he had received the year before. He'd gotten army men with their heads and arms chewed off, Hot Wheels cars with only three wheels, a transistor radio with a broken antenna that could only pick up one station, and a pair of jeans that were too small. Oh – and a football that wouldn't hold air. In fact, the only new gift he received that year was a book, a copy of *Tom Sawyer*, which he read and re-read until the cover fell off.

He tried to make the best of the toys. He pretended the army men had been in a battle, coming away with limbs missing but spirits intact. The Hot Wheels cars actually rolled pretty good as long as they were on a flat surface. And the radio – well it became one of Dean's favorites; a magical talisman that introduced him to *Casey Kasem's American Top 40* and transported him to a place far from foster care and drunken parents. It birthed a lifelong love of music that Dean never got over.

But that year on Christmas morning, Dean walked into the den and couldn't believe his eyes. There, under the tree, surrounded by the usual freight of used toys, was The Machine.

Dean never found out how his dad was able to get him the bike of his dreams, but he never forgot it either.

Excerpt from *Almost There* written by Terry D. Newberry

THE TREE

It's a real tree. Always. No exceptions. Real, evergreen, perfectly shaped. It has to be perfect. It will be the centerpiece of the Newberry great room for the Christmas season.

Getting it to the house is a family affair. Even though the girls have grown up, moved out and gotten married, it remains a family affair. Only now the family is larger and they all come back to help find the tree and decorate it.

The tradition started when Jimmy Carter was President. Nan and I were dating. When I showed up, her folks saw a young man who was interested in their little girl and they made a decision. He will be the one who goes with her to pick out a tree.

I didn't understand their decision until about 6 hours into the tree-hunting experience. We had been to every tree lot in Mobile County, Baldwin County and the Mississippi Gulf Coast. We were on our way to Pensacola to see what they might have over there when Nan decided that we should stop briefly in Mobile to take a second look at one of the trees we'd seen.

So, we returned to the very first lot we went to and wound up buying the very first tree we had looked at earlier.

Now I understood.

Thus, the tradition was born. Around Thanksgiving every year, we go in search of the perfect tree. A few times we went to an actual tree farm and cut our own tree.

But that experiment was short-lived. For openers, my bride got mad at me because I wouldn't let her wield the axe. What can I say? An angry woman with an axe? I've watched enough scary movies to realize that isn't a good idea.

And we can't forget the year when we put the lights on the tree and small bugs began to crawl out of the branches. Nan ran screaming out of the room and I thought I was going to have to put her in the hospital or something.

So, it's been pretty much only store-bought trees since then.

We were dirt-poor, but we always managed to save enough for that fresh tree. We would go in search of what she called "a Rudolph tree" and my job was to grab whatever tree she pointed at, cut the netting loose, bang it a couple of times on the pavement to loosen the branches, and spin it while she looked from every angle. Meanwhile, I was getting covered with pine sap in the bargain.

Later on, when our daughters came along, they became part of the quality inspection crew. More trees to review. More netting to cut. More trunks to bang on the pavement. I'm not going to say that we looked at a lot of trees, but my biceps grew 2" during the Christmas season and my hands had pine sap on them until sometime around Easter. Do you know how tough it is to get three ladies to agree on what a perfect Christmas tree looks like?

Once the selection is made, we bring it home and put it in our fancy stand (we have gone through a few different designs over the years, especially during those memorable occasions – yes, that would be plural, as in it happened more than once – when the fully decorated tree fell over, scattering ornaments all over the room).

Once that is done, we build a fire and put on some Christmas music. (Fair warning, when "All I Want for Christmas Is You" starts playing, I'm grabbing someone to dance. One year, one of my sons-in-law was the unfortunate victim. He sorta kept his distance from me for pretty much the rest of that evening).

We have a smorgasbord of all our favorite Christmas foods, iced punch, and little Cokes (the real deal in those tiny glass bottles. None of that plastic stuff. Not at Christmas). Thus fortified, we begin decorating.

First on are the lights. Only white lights for the Newberry house. No colors. And no blinking lights. The girls around here are purists. (Although there was that one year when I covered the entire tree in multi-colored lights, all blinking like crazy while I laughed at the expressions on their faces. Now you understand why Nan wanted to wield the axe).

So, white lights go on first. Then the real fun starts.

We have an old wooden trunk that came to American with the Gillis clan when they migrated from Ireland. Or Scotland. Depends on who you ask. Anyway, it is chock full of Christmas ornaments. When we go on a trip, we generally try to buy an ornament or two to hang on the tree to remind us of our trip that year. So, we have those.

Then there are the handmade decorations, special artwork from our girls back when they were small. There are ornaments that commemorate special occasions in our life, like a new baby or grandbaby or learning to ride a bike, or a ballet recital, and so forth.

There are ornaments from places where I have traveled, like England and Russia and Chunchula, Alabama.

Then there are the special decorations to honor loved ones who now celebrate Christmas in heaven.

Each year the whole family gathers to fulfill this tradition. Even though they have families and trees of their own, the girls and their fellas are here to trim ours. It is a time of laughter, excited discussions and quiet reflection as the memories grow year by year.

At last, the time comes to crown the tree with our angel. One of the girls had the foresight to marry a young man who is tall enough to reach the highest branch and carefully set the angel, and lo! the tree is done.

It sits in its corner next to the fireplace, quietly filling our great room with its gracious fragrance – the scent of Christmas.

It reigns as the reminder of Christmases past and present and yet to come.

Sometimes I sit by the fire and consider the tree and all the miracles it holds. Miracles of friends and family and faith. Memories of Christmases gone by, and thoughts of those which lie ahead.

And there, nestled deep in the needles, is one very special ornament that I ponder. It is my duty to hang it every year. It must be hung on a special branch close to the trunk of the tree. The branch must be strong to bear the weight of this most special ornament.

It's the Christmas Nail.

The Christmas Nail

The great room, dressed in holiday best,
with a merrily blazing fire.
The sparks dancing up the chimney
in a celebration spire.
The tree in her place of honor,
with a glittering star is crowned.
Decorated with tinsel and garland
holding ornaments all around.

Some are dated, some are worn,
some are colored, others torn.
Some are costly, some are not,
some were homemade, others bought.

Some came from exotic places, where
some of us had been,
some came from strangers,
still others came from friends.

Some are carefully colored, gifts from the pen of a
child,
some are bold and colorful, others muted and mild.

Many bring back memories of years and years before;
people, places, experiences, locked behind the
Christmas door.

On and on they go, more it seems each year.
The branches bear their glittery load
in silent Christmas cheer.
And some of these treasures bring
tears to my aging eyes
as they commemorate a place or
event in my children's lives.

And quietly hanging there,
one which outshines the others by far.
Plain and unassuming,
nestled in the tree just beneath the star.

Hung close to the trunk,
on a special branch that will hold and never fail
Though groaning a bit, proudly it holds
the weight of this special Christmas nail.

The weight of the nail is a pointed
reminder of the weight He bore for me.
A gift decorated with the ribbon of
His blood loosed and flowing free.

Of the crown of thorns circling
His head, worn for all to see.
A circle of love for my family,
like the gifts around the tree.

One end of the nail is pointed,
the sharp anguish of my sin.
The other end is flattened,
the blunted pain of where I'd been.

The length which separates these two
is the distance of His heart,
The sharpened nail driven to its
blunted end birthed the gift of another start.

A silent reminder as I ponder the tree
crowned with its glowing star
that the distance between the Christ-Tree
and the Christmas Tree isn't very far...

THE WEDDING LETTER

You have been dreaming of this day since you were a little girl.

Early on, you put the world on notice that you were going to get married, have babies, and be a great mom. You have been planning this for a long time, working out the particulars and adjusting the logistics.

I remember our first discussion on the matter. I was in the driveway washing the car. It was an amazing fall day, one of those rare and perfect gifts, one of those days that stay with you for your whole life. You were outside with me, riding your tricycle up and down the driveway.

You peddled up and informed me, "Daddy, one day I want to have a baby," and then rode away, unaware that you had just sent my poor father's heart into a nosedive, crashing into complete disarray.

One minute I am happily scrubbing the rocker panels of my old car, enjoying a beautiful day with my beautiful daughter. The next minute I am brought face-to-face with the truth of just how fleeting my time with her will be.

A few seconds later you turned around and came back, a troubled expression clouding your tiny, perfect face. "But I have to be married to have a baby," you informed me.

"That's right, sweetheart," I agreed.

"But daddy, I don't want to get married and leave you and mommy. I want to live with you forever!" you exclaimed, your eyes dark and searching.

"That is a lot of worry to be carried by someone as little and beautiful as you," I suggested. "Let's not worry about that right now...there is still a lot of time before you have to make those kinds of decisions," I told you, not sure if my advice was meant for you or for me.

"OK," you said after a second, slowly peddling away. But your face told the tale. This issue wasn't resolved, not by a long shot. You would turn it over and over in your mind until you had a solution. Little did I know back then that this approach would define how you would deal with every major decision in your life.

This time, the solution came quickly. As you reached the end of the driveway, you spun the tricycle in a quick donut turn and headed back my way, peddling for all you were worth, your eyes wide and excited. Clearly you had experienced a revelation at the end of the driveway of the Newberry home.

"Daddy! Daddy! I know what we can do! I can get married, and we can have a baby. We can live with you and mommy! We can live in the attic!"

"Well, sweetheart, that is certainly OK with me," I replied, laughing.

At this point your tiny face became very serious, your dark eyes looking directly at me as you quietly informed me, "But you'll have to put a chair up there for us."

This story still brings a smile to my face and tears to my eyes. It turns out I was right, back then there was still a lot of time to make decisions. But the time has come. You have made a decision. In the words of the poet Solomon, you have found the one your heart loves.

Who can understand the mind and the plans of God, our Abba Father? Certainly not the likes of me. When your mom and I packed you off to Hattiesburg Mississippi for a new teaching job, our thoughts were focused on your career and the many lives you would impact. Our thoughts were on your safety and stability as you continued your life journey. Our hearts were filled with happiness and joy over your new opportunity, combined in equal measure with anxiety and sadness over your move.

And as that year progressed with its freight of challenges and setbacks and discouragement, I wondered. I pondered. I fussed. I fumed. I was angry. I was worried. I was sad.

I was confused. Why would God move you so far away, only to allow such difficulty in your life? And through it all, God smiled.

You see, He knew all the lives you would enrich and inspire, children and adults alike. He knew how your faith and spirit would grow. He understood that adversity breeds depth and wisdom and compassion.

But that isn't all. He had one more trick up those big sleeves of His. He had tucked your soulmate away for safekeeping – in Hattiesburg Mississippi.

I can almost see Him now as He turned to Gabriel and said, "Hey Gabe! Watch this!"

Watch this indeed. His gifts and His calling are irrevocable and perfect. Perfect in every respect – especially their timing.

Which brings us to now. You are getting married. You'll have those babies and you'll be a great mom. How do I know? Because your mom and I have watched you grow into an incredible person.

From the very beginning, your life has been fraught with challenges. A long labor, a difficult birth, and then you had to suffer the indignity of your daddy putting your very first diaper on… backward!

How can such a tiny body house such a powerful spirit? That was the question your mom and I asked ourselves over and over as you grew. You met every obstacle head on and never quit, never gave up until you came away with the prize. And today is no different, but my goodness, the prize is awesome!

Today God gives you a husband, a protector and a shield. He has given you a provider, a comforter, someone to laugh with, to yell at, to cook for and to nurture.

Your Abba Father has given you someone to pray with, to worship with, to do ministry with and to grow a family with. From the ashes of difficulty God has raised a new life for you and your soon-to-be husband.

Cherish him, protect him, share with him. Never let the truth of your marriage be tainted with the stain of deception. Be mad at him when he deserves it (which I am sure will be often ☺), but never go to bed angry. Speak your truth quietly and clearly, and listen to his truth with your ears, your mind, your heart and your spirit. Pray for him, pray with him, be his biggest fan and his most honest counselor.

And to your beloved I say this: tomorrow I will give to you my most precious treasure – one of my daughters. God has spent many years preparing her for you. She is precious. She is priceless. She is gentle and caring. She is deep.

Treasure her for the perfection she is. I charge you to protect her and care for her. I charge you to be the man God has called you to be and the husband to my little girl that He has placed within you to be.

I charge you to be the spiritual head of your household, and to take those responsibilities and duties with the utmost of focus and serious attention.

And I welcome you into the most intimate relationship I have to offer – my family. You are part of our family. You can help decorate the Christmas tree, drink little cokes with us on special occasions, and share in all our special times. I will be your friend, your prayer partner, and a father to you.

I encourage you to always celebrate one another – through the happy times like today, and the times which are not as happy, because they too will come your way.

And I charge the both of you together to be the kind of parents to your children that will teach them the way they should go. Share the truth of Jesus with them at every opportunity. Make them laugh. Make them sing. Make them proud.

Make them strong.

And be an example to others in your gentleness and care for one another.

You are on a great journey, a journey the end of which is known only to God. It is a road filled with joy and laughter that will be tempered at times by pain, loss and tears.

But you are not alone. You have each other. You have all our family. You have God the Father who even now is turning to Gabriel and saying, "Hey Gabe! Watch this!"

Go now. Go with God and know that you travel with our hearts in your pocket.

Love,
Daddio

THE WRITER

Ok, I'd heard the rumors. Apparently, some famous writer was attending our church. I don't generally pay much attention to rumors, but this was a writer, a real bona-fide published author. He had written real books that real people bought with real money so they could read what he wrote.

So, ok, maybe I looked for him a time or two in the sanctuary.

I taught an adult Sunday School class. I was in the middle of teaching one morning when he came strolling in. He and his wife sat down somewhere toward the back as a stir went through the classroom. He was here! That famous writer we been hearin' about – he's sittin' right over there!

As for me, my mouth suddenly got real dry. I tried to drum up some spit to unstick my tongue, but nothin' doing. So, I just nodded and smiled for a couple of minutes until I got things under control and back to normal.

His name was Calvin Miller. He was in fact a very published author - over 40 books, some of them best sellers.

He was a theologian, a speaker, a pastor and a professor. He was the Distinguished-Writer-in-Residence at the prestigious Beeson Divinity School at Samford University. He was a poet, an orator and a scholar.

He was my friend.

After class that day, he wandered to the front and told me how much he enjoyed the lesson. He mentioned that maybe I could come by the university sometime and we could have lunch.

Now you have to understand that generally speaking, Southern Baptists have two failings. The first, as you might have guessed, is food. The second is to be kind to folks that are struggling. So, I chalked his invitation up to a kind Southern Baptist pastor reaching out to a struggling young teacher to comfort him with food. I never followed up on the invitation.

He didn't come back to class for a couple of weeks, which reinforced my hypothesis. But somewhere around the third week, there he came, walking big as life with his bride in tow. After class he again made his way up front and waited patiently while I spoke to a handful of class members gathered there.

"Hey," he said. "You never called. Did you lose my card?"

"No sir," I replied. "I thought you were just being nice."

He smiled at me and handed me another of his business cards. "Call me," he said. "Let's have lunch this week."

Did I mention that I had a dream of writing a book? I'd written one book on the life of Joseph which had been published. Working on that book had whetted my appetite to do another one.

So, I called the number on Calvin's business card. His secretary booked an appointment and bade me show up 15 minutes early. Which I did.

I dug through my closet and found my best tie, knotted it in the tightest half-Windsor I could manage, and headed to Calvin's office.

He greeted me like I was an old friend. He introduced me to his secretary, a couple of other professors and a graduate student or two.

He made me feel like he was showing me off, like I was a long-lost friend come back for a visit, and he felt happy to be spending some time with me and wanted everyone to know it. He made me feel like I was his best friend.

He was Calvin.

We walked across campus and several people stopped us to chat and ask him for an autograph. Each time, he stopped and greeted the person.

He introduced me and then asked them a few questions about where they were from, what they were planning to do in the future, that sort of thing. Questions to put them at ease.

He then pulled a fountain pen from his jacket and signed their book or napkin or whatever with the most beautiful calligraphy you've ever seen.

He then capped his pen, told them how much he enjoyed meeting them, and on we went to lunch.

He took me to the Staff lunchroom which was a pretty fancy affair with white tablecloths and white cloth napkins.

There was a feast at hand; southern cooking like fried chicken, mashed potatoes, green beans, yeast rolls, cornbread, and gallons of sweet iced tea sitting in sweating pitchers.

A server took our order and we settled into a conversation. I didn't know it then, but it would be the first of many we would have over the years.

We discussed everything from poetry to philosophy, from faith to fantasy, from love to leadership. Calvin was an accomplished writer, painter, orator, philosopher, musician, pastor, professor and leader.

He was a modern renaissance man, a visionary whose interests were varied and relevant.

On the way back from lunch, we walked the pathways meandering across the beautiful tree-covered campus. We stopped by the bookstore. The staff rushed to greet him and shake his hand. Browsers in the store came over and introduced themselves and told him how much they enjoyed his work.

It was like having lunch with Paul McCartney or something.

He was gracious and patient with everyone, and more than once his pen came out of that pocket to do a book signing. He was Calvin.

When the hubbub settled down a bit, he walked over to a book table laden with his latest best seller. There was a full-sized cardboard cutout of him next to the display, and it was a little surreal to see him standing next to it.

He grabbed a book from the pile and walked to the register. I watched, curious. He paid for the book and then walked back over to me. Out came the pen.

He autographed the book in that beautiful calligraphic handwriting of his.

"To Terry Newberry –

A brother –

A mentor –

A friend –

Calvin

He had that gift, you see. The one I told you about earlier. He made me feel like I was his best friend, that our friendship was important to him.

We continued our friendship over the years, meeting often for lunch or breakfast. He invited me to his home, and I marveled at his book collection.

I enjoyed the stories about how he wrote his best-selling trilogy "The Singer". Movie rights were being discussed. Big things happening.

He talked to me about some of my other favorite writers like Philip Yancey, Eugene Peterson and Max Lucado. He was friends with all of them and had even collaborated on books with some of them. He was pals with Ray Bradbury and so many other writers. I was like a little kid – "Wait. What? You are friends with Ray Bradbury?!" That kind of thing.

He just smiled his Calvin smile and endured my open-mouthed, sophomoric comments. He was Calvin.

We talked about spiritual things and current books we were reading, spiritual and secular. Our discussions covered a multitude of topics; writing styles, the hidden messages in some books that the reader had to dig for, the beauty of the ordinary.

He was a huge music buff, and ABBA was one of his favorite groups. We took our brides on a double-date one night to see an ABBA Tribute band on the university campus.

He remained a faithful member of our class and was there every Sunday that he wasn't traveling to speak somewhere. From time to time, I would get a note from him, telling me he enjoyed the lesson, encouraging me, guiding me. He was the consummate mentor.

Eventually the day came when I was ready to publish *"The Boss"*. I asked Calvin if he wouldn't mind too much, could he possibly find time in his schedule to write a forward for the book?

For all the years I knew him, he was always working on a deadline for a book. But that never stopped him from dropping everything when someone needed help. He wrote an amazing forward for my book. It was so good I hear that some folks bought the book just for that. They read Calvin's intro and then put the book in a drawer somewhere. No need to read past what the master wrote.

The last time I saw Calvin was at a book signing for "*The Boss*". Fitting, I think.

He and his lovely bride Barbara showed up with one of those gigantic cookies with "*The Boss*" written in chocolate icing.

He was kind enough to pose with me on that most special occasion. He knew how much it meant to me to have that book published, and how much it meant to me to have him there. He was Calvin.

He died the next week.

I was devastated. How could the world exist without Calvin Miller? Who would write powerful prose the way he did?

I went to his funeral. After all, I was his best friend, right? I had a hard time finding a place to park, although the parking lot was very large. I walked into the church and had a hard time finding a seat, although the sanctuary was enormous.

I stood in the back and listened as person after person walked to the podium and shared how Calvin Miller had affected their lives, put them on a new trajectory.

Turns out that Calvin had a lot of best friends.

He was Calvin.

WHAT SONG IS THAT

I woke up this morning with a song stuck in my head - "*Under the Boardwalk*" by The Drifters. Now that isn't really a problem I guess, except that I went to sleep singing "*Shout to the Lord*".

So how did I go to sleep focused on the Lord and wake up with a Summer Oldie running around in my head?

And while I'm on the subject, I wonder if that ever happened to Jesus? I mean, He was surrounded by the culture of His time, and that included music. Was there maybe a "Top 40" band in Nazareth that had a hit with a killer hook that just got stuck in his brain?

I know some of you are saying, now hold on Terry, you've crossed the line. This is Jesus we're talking about! Relax, I am not trying to be disrespectful or sacrilegious, but I mean, let's be honest here. Don't you think that maybe that happened sometimes?

Music has always been a big part of my life. When I was a kid, and I'm talking like 8 or 9 years old, I have a clear memory of hearing *"You Can't Hurry Love"* by the Supremes.

The girls who lived next door, Tammie and Cindy, had a little portable record player. I had a crush on both of them (even at such a young age I aimed high) and spent as much time as possible at their house.

One day we were on their carport playing 45's, and that song came on. I was hooked. (Funny story, when my grandson was born, we were all in the hospital waiting room and it was taking forever! Those of you who have had the experience of waiting for a little one to make his or her grand entrance to the planet know exactly what I am talking about.

I was praying that everything was going OK with mom and baby, and I was fretting in my prayer about how long this was taking. Right in the middle of my prayer, from the overhead speakers I heard the unmistakable bass and tambourine intro of the Supremes *"You Can't Hurry Love."* I laughed, and thanked God for the message and the humor of His delivery).

Did you see what I did there? His delivery? Get it? Never mind!

Anyway, as a kid, I had friend who lived across the street. His name was Johnny. His sister was Denna, and she was a huge fan of the Monkees.

Their stereo was the real deal, a big console job with a turntable, radio, and gigantic speakers. I spent many happy hours in their den listening to that 1960's-era cutting edge audiophile equipment and learned all the words to every Monkees hit.

I proudly stood on my stage (the ottoman in their living room) singing into my microphone (his sister's hairbrush), imagining that I was Davy Jones. (Years later I got a chance to meet Davy and it was surreal, let me tell ya.)

Music became my escape, and by 1967, the year I turned 10, I was a hardcore music guy. I became enamored with the drums. A kid in my neighborhood had a 4-piece Ludwig Downbeat drum set done up in Oyster Blue Pearl. I used to go to his house to listen to him play. At school, I drew pictures of drum sets on my work papers and got a couple of rulers across the knuckles for my troubles.

When I hit my teen years, Casey Kasem was my hero. On Sunday mornings I'd get up early, grab my little 9-volt transistor radio (used, courtesy of some Child Services toy drive for foster kids), hop on my bike and head to my hideout.

The antenna on the radio was broken, but if I tilted it just the right way, I was rewarded with the sound of Casey's voice spinning the hits and telling me all about the artists who recorded them. For a few hours each Sunday, I was as free as the music floating unseen through the airwaves.

There was a small corpse of woods not too far from the home I lived in. In it was my secret hideout no one knew about. It was a place where I was safe, wrapped in the good sounds of The Rascals, Cream, Simon and Garfunkel, The Grass Roots, Tommy James and the Shondells and the Beatles.

I knew all the artists and all the lyrics. "Hey Jude" and "Let It Be" ruled the airways.

So, like many of you, music was the soundtrack to my life. My kids laugh at me these days because a song will come on the radio and I will cite artist, title and year – and tell them what grade I was in at the time the song came out. It tickles me that they enjoy some of the same music that I did growing up.

When I was a high school freshman, I got my first real job (Thom McCann, shoe salesman). With my very first paycheck I bought my mom a set of china dishes, and a little stereo with a turntable for myself. And my first album purchase? The Beatles, of course. "Let It Be".

I still have that album (and in case you were wondering, one of my daughters still has the dishes), and I have added many more records to my collection over the years.

My sweet bride bears my hobby (I have asked her to stop using words like "bankruptcy" and "obsession" and "lunacy") with patience and grace. My tastes evolved over time and my music room has a wide selection of Jazz, contemporary Christian, Classical and of course, Rock and Top 40.

Music remains vital to me although I am careful what I listen to because I have to protect my mind, and as you all know, there is a lot of opportunity in today's music to pollute our minds – be careful little ears what you hear, right?

I go to sleep pretty much every night meditating on scripture or singing a worship song. There have been many occasions when I awoke in the middle of the night and the first thing I was aware of was a worship song playing in my mind. How awesome to think that while my body is resting, my spirit is worshipping.

But sometimes, a little ditty by the Drifters creeps in. I always apologize to the Lord, but you know what?

I think He understands.

WHEN YOU TALK TO ME

She had a quick break between classes and needed to visit the ladies' room. That last soft drink from lunch was demanding attention.

From beyond the closed door of the stall she heard the voices of a couple of girls who were no doubt also feeling the demand of a soft drink or two. After a moment she recognized their voices. It was two of her friends.

She was about to wrap up business and surprise them when she heard one of them mention her name.

Who doesn't want to hear what people say about us when we aren't around? Like Huck Finn and Tom Sawyer hiding in the church gallery to spy on their own funeral - it's just too tempting to ignore. So, she sat very still and very quiet.

Unaware that the object of their discussion was at the present moment sitting less than 10 feet away, one of her friends said some things about her that were very hurtful, shocking even. And completely untrue. And the thing of it was, the girl who was telling the tales *knew* they weren't true. Shocked, she waited for her other friend to come to her defense. Wait, here it comes! My friend will set the record straight and tell the truth.

The other friend not only didn't come to her defense, she added a little more gossip to the mix. They chatted for a few minutes like a couple of old maids chewing on an especially tasty bit of muck.

It seemed like they talked forever, although it could only have been a few minutes. It didn't take too long. The dark rhythm of their words left their lips and like a tornado set about destroying everything good that stood in their path. The girls washed their hands, and tossed the paper towels into the trash, along with the dreams of their wounded friend, and left the washroom.

She fought back tears at first, weeping silently, shoulders shaking against the sudden loneliness. Her world crashed down all around her, dreams shattering on the dirty tiles of a high school toilet. All alone in an empty toilet stall.

But she didn't weep silently for long. As soon as the girls left, she burst into sobs, doubled over by the power of the betrayal. Grief and anger and disillusionment rose in a dark cloud, obscuring her light.

And that took some doing, let me tell you. Because this kid has some kind of inner light. It is the kind of interior sun that only comes around once in a very blue moon. She is authentic beyond reproach. She is the kindest, gentlest soul you could ever hope to meet. She cares about others, especially those who are hurting or defenseless. She is empathetic to the point that it sometimes brings her pain, pain felt for the plight of others. Like I say, the kid has some light.

And I should know. I'm her dad, you see.

She came home from school that day a changed person. Her interior sun was dimmed. The radiant aura she wore like a robe around her was gone. She was crushed. She was devastated. She was… diminished.

I love my daughters. They are, simply put, amazing. I have always worked hard to have a great relationship with them.

When they were small, I would call them from work and ask if they wanted to go on a date with daddy. After work, I would pull the car to the curb at our home and walk up the walkway to the front door. I would ring the doorbell and be greeted by a little princess, all dressed up for her date with Daddy.

We'd go bowling, or to McDonalds or on a picnic… didn't matter really. What mattered is that we were together. You get me, right?

So, back to my story. I arrived home after work, and my daughter wasn't in her customary place in the kitchen helping her mom with dinner. I climbed the stairs to her room and knocked on the door. "Go away," came the response from the other side, delivered in a flat, emotionless voice I had never heard from my little girl. And never wanted to hear, come to think about it. Something was definitely wrong with this picture.

"It's Dad," I said softly. "Can we talk?"

Now at this point in the story, my hurting daughter is supposed to open the door and fall into my strong daddy arms. She is supposed to cry until all the pain is cried away. I am supposed to kiss her forehead and remind her how beautiful she is and how it's time for us to go back to the time when the stars were still in reach. The light is supposed to come back into her eyes and her radiance is supposed to go back to the superbright glow of a nova. I am supposed to fix this.

But that isn't how it played out. She told me to go away. She meant it too. Turns out betrayal hurts everyone in its path. It's like the gift that keeps on giving.

Still talking through the closed door, I gently reminded her of how much I loved her and that I was always there to listen. When she was ready, we could talk.

This went on for days. My vivacious daughter was hollow-eyed and empty-hearted. She had new wisdom now, wisdom bought with the bright coin of her innocence. Her soul bore the fresh tattoo of betrayal, and that ink is permanent, baby, let me tell ya. Even daddies can't erase that stuff.

I was getting desperate. I had no idea how to breach the wall of grief and alienation. I didn't know how to piece her dreams back together, how to restore the innocence of my little girl. I prayed for wisdom. I read books. I tried to talk with her. I tried Dad jokes.

Nothing worked.

Finally, my desperation forced me to pen and paper. I wrote her a letter, pouring out my anguish in the message I wanted to tell her, but could not. Here in the scrawled language of an anxious father, I shared my heart.

The final version was tear-stained, let me tell you. Here's what I wrote to her.

When you talk to me, I will tell you that you are more beautiful and stronger than you know. I will tell you that God is using you to touch and heal the lives of others.

When you talk to me, I will tell you that you are generous and caring and touched by the hurts that you see in those around you. I will tell you that you are a natural leader, and that is sometimes a lonely place.

When you talk to me, I will tell you that you are a loyal friend, and that you are thoughtful and kind. I will tell you that not everyone you will meet in the world has these characteristics, and that the discovery of this truth is marked by a sense of betrayal, hurt, and sometimes tears.

When you talk to me, I will tell you that you are intelligent and creative. I will tell you that your mind and your heart do not always walk hand in hand, and that learning which of these to follow will be a lifelong journey.

When you talk to me, I will tell you that God has a perfect plan for you – just for you. I will tell you that before you were born, He had a perfect path laid out for you, one which is paved with both natural gifts and life experiences. The natural gifts are sometimes wild and unruly, and require careful pruning and care. The life experiences are sometimes challenging and painful, and require a perspective that comes from Him to keep things in balance.

When you talk to me, I will tell you that many people and experiences will come into your life, each bearing a chisel. The carving and shaping that they do in your life is part of God's plan to reveal the person He created you to be.

When you talk to me, I will tell you that you are competitive and ambitious, gifts that He placed within you. I will tell you that keeping these in balance, and avoiding jealousy of the accomplishments of others is a constant struggle in the life of a leader.

When you talk to me, I will tell you that you push yourself to be the best you can be, and that it pays off. I will tell you that you will not always live up to the ideals you set for yourself, and that it is important for you to be as kind and forgiving to yourself as you are with others.

When you talk to me, I will tell you that it is less important that you seek friends than it is that you seek to befriend others. I will tell you that it is more important that you seek to meet the needs of others, than to have your own needs met.

When you talk to me, I will tell you that there are many paths for a person like you who has so much to offer. I will tell you that the decisions you make should be bathed in prayer, wisdom and the counsel of others. I will also tell you that you don't have to make all your life decisions right now.

When you talk to me, I will tell you that there is no relationship more important than the one you have with God. I will tell you that as you meditate on His Word, He will shape your viewpoints, your heart and your perspective on life. I will tell you that without His Word in your life, you will find it difficult to be the person that He created you to be.

When you talk to me, I will tell you that there is no conversation more important than the one you have with God. I will tell you that as you communicate with Him, you are talking to One who knows the very number of the hairs on your head, who understands you better than anyone else, and who loves you completely, totally and unconditionally. You are covered in

His fingerprints. Your name is inscribed on the palm of His hand.

When you talk to me, I will tell you that when I look at you my heart fills and it is sometimes hard to hold back my tears. I will tell you that these are tears of gratefulness, joy, and sometimes hurt as I am a spectator to your life race.

When you talk to me, I will tell you that the world needs you and that you have made a mark on it. I will tell you that it is a better planet for having you as its citizen. I will tell you that your work here is far from done, and that you will leave an impression and legacy so great that it cannot be measured in this lifetime.

When you talk to me, I will tell you that someday you will marry the man of your dreams. I will tell you that I pray often for this man, that God will keep him pure and that he will be a man of conviction, prayer and Godliness. I will tell you that I pray he will cherish you for the perfection that you are.

When you talk to me, I will tell you that someday you will bear children, and that the spirit that now lives in you will pass to them. I will tell you that I pray often that they will come to know God as their source and their Savior and that *they will bring a sense of pride, joy and unmatched love to your life, as you have to mine.*

When you talk to me, I will tell you that I am proud of you. I will tell you that you make my heart sing. I will tell you that no matter where you are, no matter what you do, no matter what pain you experience, no matter, no matter, no matter…I will always be here.

When you talk to me, I will tell you that you are more beautiful and stronger than you know.

When you talk to me –

I love you –
Daddy

FAIRHOPE

I'm sitting in a small diner in downtown Fairhope. It's the kind of place that the locals know. The kind of place where the home fries start their lives as actual potatoes.

They serve cat head biscuits and omelets hot off the grill, big around as your wrist and chock full of chunky vegetables and onions and bacon and ham. The cheese pulls when you cut into it and follows your fork all the way to your mouth, forcing you to grab it between your fingers to break the cheesy pull.

There's just no elegant way to eat an omelet here.

The coffee is hot, and the cups are bottomless. There is a quiet hum of conversation; only a few early risers, up before the dawn, sprinkled through the dining room with its metal chairs and Formica tabletops.

The place is pretty much unchanged since I was last here. I came through a few years ago on a long weekend sabbatical / bicycle trip during a time when I needed to clear my head and seek wisdom about an important decision.

On that trip I spent the days cycling the winding two-lane that meanders along the contours of the bay, smelling in turn the magnolias and jasmine and the fecund fragrance of the bay.

Before I started my daily cycling, I began each morning here, in this same small restaurant, in the last booth way back in the corner. Back then there was old-school country music coming from the overhead speakers; George Jones and such. Today, it's a Top 40 mix with some Adele and Kelly Clarkson.

Other than that, not much has changed. Even COVID didn't affect it too much; the salt and pepper shakers sit right there on the table side by side with the jellies and cream and sugar stacked neatly in their plastic bowls. Don't see that much anymore.

It's the kind of place where the old timers gather every morning to sip hot coffee and talk weather and politics. Not so long ago the conversation included farming and crops but seems a lot of the farmland around here is growing condos these days.

When I walked in, the old timers gave me the once-over and then went back to their coffee and quiet conversation. They didn't know quite what to make of me with my jeans-and-sport coat attire, longish hair, and earring.

I guess I can't blame them too much; I don't know what to make of me these days either. The last time my hair was this long Richard Nixon was crooking his way through the presidency. It has grown over my collar and beyond. My bride tells me I look shaggy.

My family is pretty sure I am going through a mid-life crisis. I hope that is true. If this is mid-life that means I am going to live until I'm one-hundred-twenty-something. Imagine how long my hair will be by then.

I'm in town taking care of some family business. I was asked to be the executor of my in-laws' estate and I naively agreed. I love them and appreciate the trust they placed in me when they asked if I would do this, but I gravely underestimated the complexity of the endeavor. And by the way, why does it take my attorney a week to return a call?

I've been down on the coast frequently over the past few months and an interesting thing has happened. I am homesick.

We left Mobile over 25 years ago. A quarter-century has passed since I last called this place home. I worked for Ma Bell, and she decided it was time for us to move. We pulled up roots, sold our home and a few stray belongings that wouldn't fit on the moving truck, and high-tailed it to Birmingham in answer to her call. Eventually, we moved to Atlanta, which these days is where we call home.

I've been back to Mobile any number of times since I left. I love the spirit of the place; there is something ancient and mysterious about it. There are centuries-old oaks with Spanish moss dripping from their branches and antebellum homes lining the streets. There is *Carpe Diem*, the finest coffee shop on the planet if you ask me, and the waterfront with its busy to-and-fro of ship traffic.

When I was a kid, I worked downtown close to the river terminals and saw that ship traffic up close and personal. I remember watching as they built the twin tunnels, boring under the river like a double-barreled shotgun.

I was around when they built the Mobile Auditorium with its futuristic design, as round as a pie plate. And I saw them build the First Federal Bank building, which was the tallest thing on the skyline back then, looking like some fabled tower to heaven.

I remember the peanut man who plied his trade in the middle of Government Street by the old cannon, and the nut shop over on Dauphin by the Square that filled all of downtown with its fragrance of roasting peanuts. I was in there not long ago and told the kid behind the counter about how I used to come in there when I was a kid myself, and about all the things that had changed since then. He stifled a yawn and asked if I wanted a co-cola to go with my peanuts.

Then there was The Haunted Bookstore and Korbets and The Captain's Table. I remember Woolsworth and Gayfers and Delchamps and Kress, all names which have vanished from the marketplace.

I remember when Fairhope was just a sleepy dream on the Eastern Shore. That was a long time ago before folks discovered how amazing it is and began to flock there by the score.

But I digress. Like I said, I am homesick. Over the years I came back to Mobile time and time again with no discernable heart tugs when I left and crossed the twin bridges headed north. It wasn't home anymore. It was just a place I used to live.

But something has happened to me during these recent months. Maybe it's the same thing that made me get an earring and let my hair grow. I feel the siren song of change in my soul; the gravity of home.

I feel the pull of the bay and the tug of the moss-draped oaks. I feel the need to sweat in the warm humid air that is part of every month except maybe a few days in December. I feel the need to bear witness to the blooming of the azaleas and the smell of jasmine in the spring.

I am drawn to sunsets on the bay; the kind where the sun seems to slip slowly into the water and folks gather on the piers to mark this daily magic with a quiet "aahhh" as it disappears below the rim of the horizon. I want to smell fish frying in the waterside cafes. I want to listen to Catt's Sunday Jazz brunch on WZEW, like it was meant to be.

I want to sail the waters of the bay and visit the lighthouses up close and in person. I want to shop the antique stores and bookstores and music stores that line the streets of Fairhope. I want to have a cup of coffee and sit outside Page and Palette to people watch.

I want to visit May Day Park and sit at my favorite table to write my stories, my ears filled with the sound of birdsong and the waves lapping the shore in patient insistence. I want to feel the peace and wonder of this place as I sit in a swing beside the water, rocking gently in the breeze that comes off the water to cool the sweat from my face.

I want to watch the fishermen cast their nets in the twilight, silhouetted against the purple and red sky of the gloaming; to hear the laughter and happy cries of small children running along the shoreline and playing in the sand while the tea-colored water of the bay laps at their feet.

I want to watch lovers stroll along the length of the pier, fingers entwined, lost in one another and the magic of all that surrounds them.

While I was in town this time, I decided to ride by the small house I shared with my friend Jerry during my college days. He was my roommate and the bass player for the band I traveled with for over a decade. We lost him two years ago this month, and that loss still surprises me with its guerilla ambushes; his memory shows up at the most unexpected times. I miss him fiercely.

Turns out that the house is no longer there. Only an empty lot. But the tree we used to park under all those years ago still stood serene, only a bit older. Like me.

I'm a bit reflective these days I suppose. I'm beginning to understand that while the first part of our life is all about gain, the back half of our life is often riddled with loss.

I've lost several members of my family and some good friends over the past few years. I've battled cancer. I've watched the world implode as I shake my head at the foolishness around me.

But I've also met people who inspire me with their life story, their art, their craft, their words, their music, their approach to this thing called life. Some of them have lived through the most hellacious existence imaginable, and yet they get up every single day with a prayer on their lips and praise in their hearts. They attack the day with a sense of wonder and humor that defies all rational explanation.

So, I'm not sad, or depressed, or hopeless. Only reflective. I am as excited about life as ever. I used to be a rock-n-roller and had long hair. I never had the nerve to get an earring, but the desire was always there. And I was a corporate guy, so the hair was all business.

But now, I am older, and I guess it's okay if I grow my hair while I still have it and get an ear piercing.

And it's ok to be reflective.

See, I have a hope inside me that cannot be quenched by the circumstances of this life. My hope is one of eternity, of a Father who loves me and knew me even while I was being formed in my mother's womb.

He knows the number of hairs on my head, even when they turn grey or I've let them grow a little longer than normal. I am covered in His fingerprints. My name is inscribed on the palm of His hand.

So, as I sit here next to the bay with its gentle waves and soaring birdsong, I want to pray in this place where I somehow feel closer to God. Heaven seems closer here as it touches the face of the water. Maybe prayers move faster when there is nothing to interfere with their journey from our heart to His.

And maybe it's because although I know He is everywhere, if I was Him, I would live in Fairhope.

Halloween

When I was a kid, Halloween was a pretty big deal. Our costumes were home-made and we carried brown paper sacks to stash our loot.

Some of the houses in the neighborhood handed out freshly baked cookies and brownies and such. Some of them gave great candy like Hershey bars. Although, to be completely honest, I have to tell you there were a few cheapskates that gave out hard candy. And just to clear up any confusion, there was a direct correlation to the kind of candy you gave out and the chances of your house getting rolled.

By the time Halloween rolled around, summer had pretty much given up her fight, and the evenings were cool. But we wore short sleeves anyway because we worked up a sweat running from house to house. Then, as now, some folks turned off their front porch lights and chose not to participate in the festivities. Didn't bother us a bit; we still walked to the door and yelled "Trick or Treat" in our loudest voice. Sometimes we stayed there a few minutes, banging on the door and yelling at the top of our lungs just to make a point. What kind of killjoy doesn't participate in Halloween?! I mean, seriously!

The night always started with a meeting on the corner of Cadillac and Farnell in the front yard of Gail's house. They had the best yard in the neighborhood for the football games that seemed to form up pretty much every fall afternoon.

Dea, me, and sometimes Rusty and Johnny met there as the sun was starting her downward trek toward the horizon. As the shadows grew and the afternoon took on that golden light that is unique to southern afternoons, we laid out our plan of attack, which always included a costume change and a second run through the neighborhood.

As the late afternoon waned into dusk, we waited anxiously for the street lights to flicker on. Normally that meant it was time to head home for dinner and a bath. But not on this night. This night was special.

As soon as the streetlights came on, we began our initial foray. We were armed with rumors about who would have the best candy and goodies this year, and we made a beeline to those houses first. To the winner go the spoils, right?

After the first pass through neighborhood, we found a quiet place under a streetlamp and examined our take. Had to be careful during that time because your buddies would try to steal your loot. We always posted a lookout. You can never be too careful where chocolate is concerned.

Those were innocent days. But I grew up, and like many of you, I sort of lost touch with Halloween. But when my daughters came along, I rediscovered the joy of trick-or-treating.

My girls wore costumes that were usually homemade, but not in the same way ours were as kids. Back then, we made liberal use of cardboard, markers and, if we could get our hands on it, face paint. The costumes worn by my kids were more often than not hand-stitched by their mom.

Over the years they were princesses, ballerinas, the latest Disney character – all of these outfits hung in their closet at one time or another. As for me, I always dressed as a businessman, with a suit and tie. Saved time. Come home from work and I am already dressed for the night's festivities!

I remember the first Trick-or-Treat after we moved to Birmingham. We hadn't lived there long, and the girls were adjusting to the new school and new friends. They were still young enough to enjoy Halloween, and I looked forward to walking them around the new neighborhood on the big night. We dressed in our costumes, grabbed our flashlights and plastic pumpkin candy pails, and headed out.

It was a perfect fall evening. The sounds of neighborhood kids running and screaming took me back to those nights of my childhood so long ago. Nights that were in many ways just like this night.

The crisp air was redolent of the dry whispered scent of leaves sacrificed to the changing of the season. They crunched underfoot like tiny skeletons as we walked, puffing the last of their essence in shades of brown, gold and red dust that clung to our shoes.

The moon was out in full parade dress, a bloated orange face hanging just above the horizon. Its mellow glance added its own mystical illumination to the dusk, already pinpricked with dozens of tiny points of light from flashlights clutched in costumed fingers. Stars blazed overhead, as though jealous of the freedom evidenced by the erratic movement of the penlights below.

There were screams which seemed to be coming from a house just up the hill, and in a minute, I saw the cause of the ruckus. The world's smallest ballerina, a hippie with no discernable body hair, and a three-foot Frankenstein ran screaming, each in a different direction, and running behind was a bellowing creature in a black mask.

The mask covered the face and came partway down the torso of this apparition. The rest of the torso was covered by a tattered tee shirt, spotted with sweat and other stains better left unexamined. The lower extremities of this beast were covered with a pair of jeans that petered out in a series of irregular strips just below the knee. And in its hands, the creature carried a large plastic axe.

It was Mr. Freddie from down the street. Satisfied that he had given the three a fright that would last them until the next Halloween, the specter retreated to his porch. Hiding once again among the tall bushes that stood sentinel around the perimeter, he waited for his next "victim".

The muted sounds of laughter mingled with distant screams (no doubt another "creature" intent on leaving an impression on tiny minds) wove a tapestry of sound that erased 40 years in an instant.

Suddenly, I was back in the old neighborhood, running with Dea and Johnny and Mike, racing to the next house, vowing to get the biggest brownie, or the last Hershey bar, or the pack of gum that would almost certainly contain that

Mickey Mantle card I needed to complete my collection.

Running with the air cool on my face, confident in a future that I couldn't see but hoped in nonetheless, surrounded by friends that measured you, not by how much money you earned or what kind of car you drove, but by the fact that you were *you*.

The candy and treats were great. But the real magic of those long-ago Halloween evenings was hanging with your buddies. You didn't know it then, but there were memories being forged on the anvil of those crisp autumn nights, memories that would surface over and over in the years to come, bearing their freight of smiles.

There is one time in particular that sticks in my mind. I remember our plan for that year. It was presented to us in great detail by our friend Rusty. It was designed to get us even more candy – "doublin' our take" is how Rusty had put it.

Following The Plan, we dressed up in our handmade costumes and completed the first round of the neighborhood. Flush with candy, cookies and other treats that were sure to start fights with our little brothers and sisters, we went to our secret hideout, where we carefully stashed the loot.

Once that was done, in accordance with The Plan, we swapped costumes. Dea put on Rusty's, Rusty put on mine, and so on. It didn't occur to us until later that as far as the folks handing out candy were concerned; these were the very same three costumes that had already shown up once on their front porch on this faintly chilly All Saints Eve. The wise folks passing out candy at the door could spot a grift a mile away.

The truth of that finally dawned on us about the same time that old Mrs. Sawyer chased us off her front porch with a broom that had seen so much action its straw was worn nearly to the laces. The end was curved into a wicked talon from years of sweeping the driveway. It looked like the kind of broom that a witch would have trouble getting airborne – and if she did, would only fly in circles.

In colorful language she surely did not learn in Sunday School, Mrs. Sawyer promised various forms of bodily harm if she saw us creeping around again. Running from the house, we headed for safer ground. As soon as we were free from the threat of the broom, we stopped, breathing heavily, with sweat caught in our crewcuts like jewels of dew. Some of it trickled down our freckled foreheads into our eyes.

Dea turned to Rusty and said, "Great idea, brainless. She nearly killed us with that broom!" He grabbed Rusty in a headlock, and proceeded to give him an Indian burn, rubbing his knuckles rapidly back and forth on Rusty's crewcut.

Laughing, we pulled Dea off Rusty and helped them both to their feet.

"C'mon, let's go see what else we can get," said Rusty. "Maybe no one else will notice we've already been there." With that said, we set out again.

Halfway down the street, we came to the old Hutchcroft place. It was dark, except for a single dim bulb that burned at the top of the stairs leading to the front door. The yard was wild and overgrown. When we rode our bikes, we had to veer off the sidewalk that ran in front of the Hutchcroft place because bushes grew through the chain link fence surrounding the front yard. The branches covered most of the sidewalk, casting it in a dark shadow that somehow looked ominous and cave-like, even in the middle of summer.

We stood at the end of the driveway, looking at each other. We'd skipped this house on our first foray through the neighborhood but found ourselves drawn back now.

There were all sorts of rumors about the Hutchcrofts. Rumors that their house was haunted, rumors they were crazy, vicious rumors that they were Auburn fans. You know, crazy, scary, nutso stuff.

One year, the old Mrs., well into her 70's, passed out candy stark naked. There was a line of kids down the driveway eager to get a peek.

The year before, it was rumored that they gave out $1 bills. Mr. Hutchcroft worked as a printer, and he had supposedly cashed his paycheck, telling the bank teller to give it to him "all in ones". He took the stack of one-dollar bills back to his print shop and had them bound together with that sticky red stuff on one end, sorta like a notepad.

When a kid rang the doorbell, he answered the door (fully clothed, thankfully), and peeled a crisp new $1 bill off the stack and handed it to the surprised ghoul or princess. A whole dollar! The possibilities were endless.

We wondered if he would do that again this year. The Little General convenience store down the footpath at the end of the woods was a fine place to spend a dollar, and we spent the days leading up to Halloween walking up and down the aisles, dreaming up shopping lists that were all funded by a hoped-for dollar from the Hutchcrofts.

But alas, it was not to be. Turned out that the old couple were handing out hard candy. And they were both fully clothed. It was like a double whammy. We watched as the old Mrs. dropped the peppermints into our bags ("Here you go, that's one-two-three pieces for you, and you and you). The candy landed in the mostly-empty bags with a soft thump, and rattled around down there as though to rub it in that this year's take included no chocolate, no brownies, no naked old ladies, and worst of all – no dollar. It's a hard old world sometimes.

You know, in a world where sugar-laced goodies are readily available and even pass for nutritious food, I wonder if kids look forward to Halloween these days with the same breathless anticipation that we did.

I hope so.

Because of the memories.

SUPERMAN

I think he was Superman.

It all started pretty normally. He was born in a small town in Mississippi, one of nine children. From early in his life, he knew he wanted to be a military man. He fulfilled his dream, serving in both the US Navy and the Army. In fact, he joined the Navy and served in WW II before he ever graduated high school!

After the war, he went back home, completed his high school degree, and then it was off to the service again – this time the US Army. He fought in Korea, and survived the Battle of Pork Chop Hill, in which 257 of his fellow soldiers died. Only 14 men survived the first skirmishes. 14 out of 271.

Like I said – Superman.

During that battle, he received a battlefield commission promoting him to second lieutenant. He turned around and immediately led his men back up the hill, back into the thick of combat. He had neither the time nor the luxury of fear or hesitation. Ed W. "Too Tall" Freeman was a hero. A true, honest-to-goodness American hero.

Ed always wanted to be a pilot, but he exceeded the height limitations. He was "too tall" for pilot duties – hence the nickname. But Ed wasn't one to give up easily on his dreams. He had joined the military and served in two branches and two wars because that's what he wanted to do. He trusted that things would work out as they should. And sure enough, in 1955 the height limits were changed, and Ed became a pilot. He fulfilled his dream, and learned to fly.

I'm telling you; he was Superman.

Isn't it interesting how some people seem to be guided and set aside for a particular task or time? It's as though their calling – their passion – is a spark, an engine and a homing device, all in one, that moves them into their perfect place. That's how it was with Ed.

Think about it. Like I said, he survived a two-year assignment on the USS Cacapon during WWII. He then survived the Battle of Pork Chop Hill, beating the odds in which 271 men went in, and only 14 came out. And now, inexplicably, the height limit for pilot training was raised, and Ed realized his dream of becoming an aviator.

But perhaps there was something else at work here. Although Ed was already a hero, he was about to become the stuff of legend.

The date was November 11. The year was 1967. Ed W. Freeman was a helicopter pilot in Vietnam. He was nine days shy of his 40th birthday.

The area around LZ (Landing Zone) X-ray was hot. US Forces were surrounded and outnumbered by the enemy nearly 8-to-1. The brass on the ground had instructed that all helicopters were to clear the area – including the MedEvac teams.

There were wounded men – teen-aged boys, really – in the midst of that hell, watching the choppers peel off, one by one, each turn of the rotor taking them further away from the wounded and damned. The boys huddled on the ground, perhaps praying for a quick end, knowing the situation was hopeless.

And then Ed showed up.

Flying a lightly armored, unarmed UH-1 Huey, he landed in the middle of that maelstrom of enemy fire, taking hits. And waiting. Waiting for some of those teenagers to be loaded onboard so that he could fly them to safety.

Again, and again, he returned, his chopper pocked with bullet holes, the Perspex windows cracked and broken, smoke billowing from the motor. Fourteen times he dropped into that caldron of Hell, until he had flown every wounded soldier to safety – all 30-plus of them. He sustained four bullet wounds during the extraction.

Ed Freeman was Superman. Ed Freeman was an American warrior. Ed Freeman was a hero.

He retired as a Major in the US Army, and went home to his wife and two sons. When he got home, I wonder how many people passed him on the street, or saw him in the market, or sold him a car or socks or fishing gear, never knowing how close they were to a living legend. How many people greeted him at the Post Office and never realized that he had his very own Post Office – the one in his hometown had been named after him. Or maybe they saw him at the grocery store, unaware of the scars he bore in his body from bullet holes, unaware of the magnificent spirit contained in that aging body. Unaware.

How many sensed the man he was? How many knew the truth of his bravery? I know of at least 30 young men who were keenly aware. I wonder what those 30 young men Ed rescued on that November day did with their lives?

I wish I could have met Ed "Too Tall" Freeman. I would have enjoyed having a glass of iced tea with him. Not to talk about the war or his heroic exploits, but just to meet the man whose spirit was so powerful that it transcended risk or danger – or even death.

Yes, death. Because Ed passed away a few years ago. His passing went relatively unnoticed, which seems wrong to me. It seems that there should have been silence and fanfare and weeping and flags flown at half mast, and maybe even a disturbance in "the force".

Because Ed was a hero.

But even Superman can die.

How many heroes do we meet every day, unaware of the immensity of their spirit cloistered in a body that has become old and frail? How much we owe these silent men and women; how much respect is due them. They have a story to tell and wisdom to share, and courage to inspire.

Learning about Ed made me want to be a better person. It made me, in some small way, want to be a hero to someone. Oh, don't get me wrong – I'm not thinking of anything like Ed did. But maybe something simple. Maybe, at the end of the day, our most powerful days are those when we are able to make a difference in the life of someone else.

And boy, we could use some of those things right now. We need a few more Supermen.

We need a few more "Ed's".

THE CLASS

I work for Ma Bell. One of the things you learn pretty quick around there is that she is prone to pick one of her kids and move them at random to a brand-new job, position, or even a new city. Any time, any place.

And that's how this story began. One morning my boss called me into his office. I didn't realize it yet, but my world was about to change.

"Terry, I have good news and bad news," he said when I sat down. "The good news is that you have been promoted. The bad news is that we are losing you here in the Mobile office – the job is in Birmingham."

I was elated. I had been working hard and was excited that my efforts were being recognized with a promotion. I was also concerned. Last time I checked, there wasn't anything up in Birmingham that made me jump for joy to be moving there. Although that changed. And that is part of this tale.

We lived on the Gulf Coast in the little town of Mobile. That's where the bay is. And Fairhope is there too. And the beach. And friends. And church.

And the guys in the band. And Catt's Sunday Jazz brunch. And fresh seafood. And my girls' schools and friends. And MeMaw and PawPaw. And Aunt Shelia. And our home that we had designed and built from the ground up, picking out every color, material and fixture. Did I mention that I wasn't jumping for joy?

We had a family meeting to discuss the move. Take the promotion, or be unemployed? Stay in Mobile or move away and risk my girls never talking to me again? Try to find another job locally or have my wife quietly kill me in my sleep?

Tough decisions.

After a lot of prayer and tears we decided to move. I think it was when we were going over our finances. When outgo exceeds income, the upshot is downfall, right?

Besides, I loved working for the phone company. The leadership and coworkers were top tier. We were doing cutting edge stuff in cellular technology. You gotta be on your game to be successful in that environment and I got a lot of satisfaction working around all the brainiacs there and seeing if I could keep up. It was all rocket science and magic.

Well, the big day finally arrived, and the movers showed up and packed a lifetime of memories in some cardboard boxes. As we pulled away from our home, following the 18-wheeler that contained every earthly possession we owned, I called my best friend and told him that this move was a lot tougher than I thought it would be.

Then I hung up before he could hear the tremble in my voice and make me turn in my Man Card.

Our new home in Birmingham was beautiful. We could see the Appalachian foothills from the dining room window, so that was something. We enrolled the girls in school and began the process of learning our way around.

We only knew one couple there; Mark and Gina. Mark was a worship leader from our church in Mobile. They had moved to serve at a church in Birmingham and did their best to help us get acquainted with the state's largest metropolitan area.

Gina did her part to help us learn our way around by drawing a detailed map of every shopping mall within a 72-hour drive, which she then gave to my bride, who immediately began to test the accuracy of the map. Her goal was to find those malls and buy a pair of shoes from each one. At one point I think MasterCard called and asked us to please leave home without it.

Mark and Gina invited us to their church, and we began to visit. Little did we know the plans that God had in store for our family in that fellowship of believers.

One day Mark called and asked if I would meet him and one of the other pastors for lunch. I hung up the phone and told Nan that they had heard about her shoe habit and wanted to talk to me about increasing our giving to the church.

Turns out they wanted me to teach a class. Mark knew I had taught a class at our church back home. Apparently, this new church was launching a satellite location at the local high school campus and needed a teacher for an adult class for a few weeks while they got their plans together.

I agreed to help out for a few weeks. That "few weeks" turned out to be nearly 20 years.

The first Sunday I showed up to teach, there were maybe 10 or 11 folks there; 14 tops. Mostly couples. I introduced myself, apologized in advance because I hadn't taught in a while and I was rusty, and then shared my heart. They were gracious and patient with me. They remained gracious and patient with me over the next two decades.

The next week, there were maybe 20 in attendance. I assumed that perhaps a teacher from one of the other classes was out, so they combined with us that week. The third Sunday, we increased again. And before you know it, we were regularly seeing 120 or more in the class. We grew so quick that they moved us to the high school band room so we could seat everyone.

Some of the church leaders got nervous that we were starting a cult or something, so we baked them some casseroles, fried some chicken, and rounded things off with fresh banana pudding and a few gallons of sweet tea for the staff luncheon. When they saw the food, they realized we were still Baptists and they settled down.

Did I mention the folks in our class were awesome? They attended class faithfully, paid attention, and even took notes. And most remarkable of all, they took care of each other. In a class that size, we knew it would be easy to get lost, so we organized into Care Groups of around 10 people each, set up some administration for contacts, needs, communication, visitors, and so on. We came up with a class directory. And we continued to grow, numerically and more important, spiritually.

When there was a need, it was met. Many were the times when someone who was down on their luck found a few sacks of groceries on their front porch. Many were the times when someone with a financial need found an envelope stuffed with cash in their mailbox. We cleaned houses together. We mowed yards. We moved furniture. If someone was in the hospital, the Care Leaders let me know right away so I could go visit.

The importance of those visits came home to me when I had to be hospitalized suddenly. My bride called Gail, the class communications guru, to let her know we were headed to the emergency room. When we got there, folks from the class were waiting for us. Some of them took our daughters home and others stayed with Nan while the doctors put me through some tests. And for the few days I was there, I had a constant stream of visitors.

It was my first time in a hospital, and I just wish someone would have told me the opening in hospital gowns is supposed to be in the back. Guess that's why most of the visits were short... but live and learn, right?

My doctor told me they had to add additional staff to answer the phones at the hospital because so many people were calling to check on me. He said that he had personally received a call or two telling him to make sure he took good care of me. All this interest in my well-being kinda blew his mind until I explained to him that I owed all those folks' money.

Our class experienced some of the highest of highs and the lowest of lows. Like the time I was teaching about prophets. I brought rolls of toilet paper, tape and colored markers. We split into groups and each group dressed a poor "volunteer" as a prophet, using TP and tape. Or there was that time we were talking about spiritual attacks and I brought Silly String and squirted class members with it. Good times.

And there were some tough times. Really tough. We stood together and cried together as we buried friends, parents, spouses, and on several horrific occasions, children.

They were full of surprises, that class. Once, I told them the story of a GI Joe frogman I got one Christmas as a kid. I put him in the drainage ditch behind our house so he could swim, and that's the last time I saw him. I guess he's doing his frogman thing somewhere in the Gulf of Mexico these days.

A few weeks later I was teaching when - you'll never believe this – a real live frogman walked into the room. A full-on scuba diver showed up in class, complete with wetsuit, mask, regulator, tanks – and even flippers. He high-stepped toward me and the breath through his regulator sounded like Darth Vader was in the house. In his hand was a gaily wrapped Christmas gift which he handed to me. I opened the gift and to my surprise and delight there was a GI Joe Frogman. The class had scoured the internet and found a replacement for me.

Another time, for my birthday they got me M&Ms. Apparently, I mentioned somewhere along the way that M&Ms were my favorite. So, here I am, teaching one morning when the classroom door opens and in walk a couple of folks wheeling a brand-new industrial-size trash bin. You know, one of those big jobs with the rear wheels and the lid that will give you a concussion if it hits you in the head.

It was filled with M&Ms. To the brim. To the brim. Yeah, seriously.

Every shape, size and flavor imaginable. Peanut, Coconut, Plain, Brownie, Chocolate Popcorn, Crispy Chocolate, Almond, Raspberry, English Toffee... wrapped in candy shells (melts in your mouth, not in your hand) of reds, greens, browns, blues, yellows... you name it. There must have been 100 lbs. of those bad boys. There were even aqua colored ones. That was aqua'd, let me tell ya. (Sorry, sorry! Please don't unfriend me!)

The class was laughing and cheering as they watched me lift bag after bag in amazement. 1 lb. bags. 2 lb. bags. Boxes. More bags. Mixed bags. Regular sizes and even some of those tiny teaser packs that just leave you mad and wanting more.

I turned to the class and held up my hand. "Guys, thank you so much, what an awesome gift!" They cheered. "However, I have some bad news," I said. They got really quiet. "My doctor said I can't eat M&Ms anymore - too fattening." You could feel the air leave the room as the entire class let out a collective sigh.

"But," I said as I quickly flipped one of the peanut M&M bags upside down, "He didn't say I couldn't eat W&W's!" The class broke out into laughter and wild cheers. Like I said, amazing people. (By the way, it took me nearly a week to eat all those M&Ms!)

I've sat with them at hospitals. I've been with them when they received the terrible news of a loved one's death. I've been awakened by knocks at my door or phone calls in the wee hours of the morning. I've stood by their beds and with them as they drew their last breath on this planet and their first one in heaven. I've preached their funerals and when my mom died, a bunch of them showed up to help me bury her. They drove four hours from Birmingham to be there for our family. Who does that?

I've done a wedding or two, rejoiced with them when their kids and grandkids were baptized, helped some of them find their way to Jesus, and eaten more than my fair share of their cooking.

And one time, we all went on a cruise to Cozumel together. There were like 60 or 70 of us. Matching shirts and everything. (Don't worry, I asked our folks not to wear the class tee-shirt to the ship's bar when they were meeting up with their Methodist buddies). It was like being part of the biggest field trip ever. We had Bible studies every day and the whole ship was invited. I even got heckled.

I love these people.

And they loved me and my family. Countless acts of kindness, notes of encouragement, birthday parties, Christmas parties, visiting the sick together, helping do house repairs or lawn maintenance together, praying together, laughing together.

They were there when my girls graduated from middle school. And high school. And college. They were there when I gave my daughters away to deserving young men at the wedding altar. And when I choked up and couldn't finish reading the letter I wrote for my daughter and her beau at the rehearsal dinner, one of the men from the class stood up, took the letter and finished reading it. With his arm around my shoulders.

Then there was the time when Ma Bell was threatening to move me to Atlanta. I asked the class to pray that God would give me clarity about what I should do. Later that night I happened to glance out the window and there standing on my lawn in the freezing rain were a dozen or so people holding hands, head bowed. Their prayers rose to heaven frosty plumes as they lifted their hearts, interceding for my family. (I got to stay in Birmingham.)

Once one of my daughters asked me, "Daddy, what would we do if we didn't have your Sunday School class?" I had no answer for her. Still don't. The magnitude of the love of those folks still awes me after all these years. Every day I want to shout or call them or email them or send smoke signals and tell them I love you guys. Always have, always will.

One day, Ma Bell reached out again, and this time I had to accept her call. With heavy hearts, we once again packed our things in boxes and followed a different 18-wheeler to a new home. This time in Atlanta.

There are no words to describe the grief of that move. Truth be told, we are still grieving. You never get over a love like that.

My birthday that year was one of those beautiful fall days, cool, with leaves of gold and red and brown drifting lazily to the lawn and spreading their fragrance like incense. I was miserable. I had been dreading that day. The class always threw a big party for my birthday and their absence cut me like a knife. My heart ached.

But there wouldn't be a party, not this year. We didn't live there anymore. They had a new teacher now.

But just about that time the first car pulled in my driveway. And the second. And the third. And so on. Then the bus. They drove from Birmingham to Atlanta to see us.

It seems there was going to be a birthday party after all.

New Orleans

New Orleans is a secret city. She guards her secrets under a shroud of beauty; lacy ironwork, ornate doors of every style, each discretely locked against the outside world. She attracts with her loveliness, binds with gentle threads of nonchalance.

She sings songs of the skillful victim, gentle arpeggios of one yearning for rescue; she promises her heart and soul to the one who can wield the sword of her delivery, the *katana* of her fate.

Her hidden alleyways open into courtyards lush with vegetation and the sound of fountain pools, surprising in their welcome and cool beauty. The sound of water is hypnotic, the air is scented with her seduction. Stay with me, she says, let's play. Tell me what you want.

Her faces are pleasing and ever-changing. Just relax, she says, let me be all you ever wanted; tell me your secrets and your loves and your passions and your lusts. Let me be all to you, and you be all to me.

Close your eyes, feel me wrapped around you, let me in.

I will give you whatever you desire, she says. But at what price, you ask – oh-never-you-mind, she replies. Just let me take care of you.

Centuries old brick paves streets which are never quite dry, but wet; baptized by the morning cleansing done as a daily ritual against the stains of the night before. Baptized by rains which come, at times in a gentle mist, sometimes in a torrent, as though the gods have tired of the stench and filth of the Quarter, and have decided to take matters into their own hands.

Sometimes these streets, witness to countless days, are washed by the waters of the river which acts as border guard, but which on occasion turns redcoat and floods the very place that the currents protected just the day before.

New Orleans is a secret city. She is treacherous without warning. Her many windows are shuttered with wooden boards, painted every color imaginable; like wooden cataracts over windowed eyes; shutters to keep the outsiders out – or perhaps to keep the insiders in. The maze of streets, each so different from the other, each so much the same, marches on in a pattern of squares and angles, seemingly to create order from the chaos of the wetlands. But the truth is far more insidious; the squares and angles confuse, double back on themselves, create dead-end eddies and places where the visitor is unwelcome.

Turn a corner at the wrong place and suddenly the world has tilted on its axis; gone are the civil and stately buildings, well maintained against the encroaching tide of the decrepit. In their place are rotting corpses of the erstwhile homes of the well-to-do; porches sagging, impaled by tall weeds growing between the floorboards.

Shutters hanging askew like the leering eyes of evil; windows broken, jagged edges of glass punctuating the stifling silence which is broken only by something rustling in the undergrowth.

Even the sound of traffic seems far away and muted; somehow veiled by the essential *wrongness* of this place. Doorframes lean drunkenly, void of the doors which once gated the entrance to the light once housed here.

Doors ripped from hinges by those seeking fuel for a fire on a cold night, by treasure seekers who come like tomb raiders, and sometimes by the winds, rebellious and foreign, which send tentative fingers to test the strength of the guards – and finding it lacking, rip them from their frames and send them screaming into the night.

New Orleans is a secret city. She speaks words pleasant to the hearing and filled with surface promise. Words expressed in the gentle accent of the southland, with soft edges and razored underbelly. Words with no meaning except to fill the void of the expected; words never intentioned to become reality. Words that captivate and beguile, words that lull defenses into a catatonic stupor of belief. Words that set the hearer up for the kill with promises of a future unfettered by worry or loss.

She lures with the scent of gardenias and lilac and blooming things. She entices with the smells of unmatched cuisine, hot and spicy and brimming with spice and ingredients foreign and exotic. But these fragrances are underlaid with the scent of things dead and dying, the intensity of which ebbs and flows like the treacherous river which acts as her border, her guard, and sometimes her destructor.

New Orleans is a secret city. She keeps you waiting with promise of what is to come; something just around the corner, something down the block, something beautiful not yet quite framed up, but marketed with glossy pages and skillful intent. She is an old hand at this; many are those who have been beguiled by thought of what might be, what *could* be.

Dreams skillfully planted and carefully tended, dreams with shiny, show off topsides and dry, crusted undersides. Dreams frayed around the edges from being handled by those to whom such future was promised. Dreams financed with the heart blood of those foolish or hopeless or desperate enough to believe.

New Orleans is a secret city....

THE POET

April is National Poet's Month.

I love that.

I love it because my earliest attempt at writing was poetry. I was 8 years old, a fresh refugee in the primitive foster care system of the day. I was in a new place, with a new "family", new surroundings, new school, new everything.

I didn't know it then, but I was learning the ropes of what it meant to be a foster kid. It meant reinventing myself every time we moved to a new place. It meant never really knowing who I was to be, because I was too busy trying to fit into the expectations that others had of me.

Pat Conroy voiced it best; *"Each year I began my life all over again. I knew no one well, least of all myself, and it damaged me, I think. I grew up not knowing if I was smart or stupid, handsome or ugly, interesting or inspired. I was too busy reacting to the changing landscapes and climates of my life to get a clear picture of myself. I was always leaving behind what I was just about ready to become. I could never catch up with the boy I might have become if I had stayed in one place."*

Amen to that.

I identify with his assessment. As I began to find my way in this new world of foster care and new schools, new friends, new everything, I discovered writing.

My second-grade teacher, Mrs. Poe, was the one who gave me the keys to this wondrous new place. One of her assignments to us on a lazy afternoon in early summer, circa 1965, changed my life. She asked us to write a poem.

I can still see it in my mind's eye.

Approximately 20 youngsters grasping a pencil in one chubby hand; 20 innocent heads bowed over 20 old-fashioned desks. You know – the ones with the small table attached to the seat and a small book cubby beneath. The smell of freshly sharpened No.2 pencils hung in the warm air. The light streaming through the windows illuminated dust motes parachuting to wherever it is dust motes go.

There, under the watchful eye of Mrs. Poe, 20 kids sat wrestling with their first exposure to that wondrous, frustrating, misunderstood, inexplicable, unforgettable thing called poetry.

My first poem was short and to the point. I still remember it. I can't remember what I had for breakfast this morning or any of the vast number of Honey-do's I have on my list and sometimes I forget the names of my children. But I remember the poem:

> *If I had a money tree*
> *Everybody would like me*
> *But I don't*
> *So they won't*

Those 16 words opened a new world for me. Poetry. The rhythm of the words, the magic of the structure, the mystery of finding words that would rhyme and at the same time make sense... all of it appealed to me.

Check that. Make that *appeals* to me.

Because I still love poetry. As a drummer, the rhythm of the phrases and words resonates with my inner metronome. The challenge of finding the perfect word and the perfect rhyme appeals to the overachiever in me. The flow of the words and the emotion they evoke appeals to the romantic in me.

I had my first work published when I was 16 years old. I placed 2nd in the Alabama State Poetry Society annual writing contest. The guy who placed first wrote a little ditty about wine and drinking and such. I never forgave myself for getting second place, so I determined I would be a better writer.

People ask me sometimes how they can become a writer. My answer is short and to the point. If you wanna be a writer, write.

So, I wrote. Over time that led to short stories, essays, more poetry, and ultimately, to writing books.

I remember clearly how it felt to hold the galley copy of my first hardback. I remember how awkward it felt the first time someone asked me to sign their book, and if we're being honest here, it still feels a little odd to pen a few words on the title page and sign a book for a perfect stranger.

Sometimes it is downright humorous. A while back I delivered a guest lecture at Auburn University where my daughter teaches.

Afterward, one of her students approached me and asked for an autograph for her dad. She excitedly explained that he had all my books and was a big fan.

After I signed her book and she left with her treasure, I told my daughter that the poor girl was confused and maybe thought I was Stephen King or something, and I hoped her dad wasn't too disappointed when she handed over the book, signed by someone he'd never heard of.

Through all the other writing, I kept penning poems. I keep a small leather journal of words and phrases that resonate with me, and sometimes they find their way into a poem. Poetry covering all sorts of topics winds up in my little notebook, and Iambic pentameter and rhymes rule.

But gradually, prose began to creep in to my work. It didn't rhyme. There was a unique rhythm to each piece. Each word stood on its own, not so dependent on its surrounding family of verbs and nouns and adjectives. Each phrase was more powerful. There was less punctuation, and in some cases, none at all. Lowercase font ruled.

March was National Women's Month and in celebration of that I began a series of short prose pieces, little vignettes if you will, that will ultimately become a book about the heart of women. You may have seen a couple of those pieces floating around Facebook. Here are a few, to help you get a sense of them:

her beauty is not just
the surface
for the uncommitted to enjoy -
it is a deep
stain of
grace

---

he thought he
knew her
but it was only
a shadow she
threw

---

her children call
her blessed
as they examine
the fingerprints
she left on their soul

I know some of my buddies from my days of
weight lifting and martial arts just threw up a little bit
and are even now calling for me to surrender my man
card.

Trust me guys, I get it. But the words come
and I am just the scribe.

One day, when my journey here is done, my
children and grandchildren will perhaps find the

reams of doodles and notes and scraps of prose and look at one another and say -

He was a poet.

THE PENNY

Dean was a high schooler working in a fast-food joint to earn some extra cash. Dates and college savings kind of stuff.

He noticed that sometimes there was food left over when the restaurant closed. Occasionally he would take a few pieces of chicken to have for lunch at school the next day, but he wondered where the restaurant leftovers went.

His question was answered one night when Sid said, "Hey, we need to make a detour on the way home."

"Sure," said Dean. "Where are we headed?"

"To the mission downtown."

Dean knew the mission. He sometimes went there to help man the food line or drop off donations. It was located in a scary part of town, a beacon of light in an otherwise decrepit and decaying part of the world.

"Ok," Dean said uncertainly. "But have you ever been there at night? It's sort of a spooky place."

"I know," Sid replied. "Someone from the store goes there pretty much every night."

This was new information to Dean.

"Why?" he asked.

"To take food. At the end of each day, we take all the food that we didn't sell and give it to the mission. They feed the hungry and homeless who come there."

"What a great idea!" Dean said. "I always wondered what happens to the food that is left over."

"And now you know," said Sid. "Dad started doing this not long after we opened. It's kind of a cool story."

"I'm listening."

"OK, one night, as we were closing up, an old beat-up car pulled into the parking lot. We could see a man and a woman in the front seat. In the back seat there were two kids. The man came to the front door. He was obviously homeless. He told us his family was in the old car, and asked if we had any food, because his children hadn't eaten in two days."

"What did you do?" Dean asked.

"At first, Dad didn't say a word. He walked to the car and looked in. I remember it was really cold that night. Dad was in shirtsleeves, and I could see his breath frosting the air as he stood by the car. It seemed that he looked at the family for a long time. Finally, he opened the car door and asked the woman,

'Would you and the children like to come in and warm up, and have something to eat?' They got out of the car and came into the restaurant."

"We had already thrown away all the food we hadn't sold. So, Dad asked each of them to order anything they wanted off the menu. While they waited on the food, we gave the parents some hot coffee, and The Boss made hot cocoa for the kids. We cooked their orders and served it to them right in the front dining room. After that, Dad made two of the biggest ice cream cones I have ever seen, and gave them to the two kids. I still remember the look on their faces. "Then Dad cooked a batch of chicken for them, because he knew it would keep for a day or so.

"When they finished eating, Dad gave them some money, and one of his cards. He told the man that if he ever needed anything, to give him a call.

"When they drove off, Dad stood in the parking lot for the longest time, just looking in the direction they had driven. When he came back into the store, he said, 'I wonder how many kids are going to bed tonight without food.' And that was it.

The very next night he delivered the first food, and as far as I know, we have never missed a night. Even on holidays like Christmas or

Thanksgiving when we are closed, he makes sure that someone cooks and delivers the food to the mission."

"That must cost a lot of money," said Dean.

"It does," Sid replied. "I asked Dad about that one night. He said the benefit of helping others outweighs the cost every time."

Dean thought about people he knew that he could have helped, but somehow never got around to it.

Feeling a little guilty, he said to Sid, "Well, I am sure it is easier to help others if you have money or something else to give them."

"Dad would probably disagree with you on that. When we were kids, we didn't have much. There were seven of us, and mom stayed at home to take care of us. A single income, nine people you can do the math.

"Anyway, one day, I got into a fight with Julie, one of my sisters. She wanted to play with a toy I got for Christmas, but I was afraid she might break it. She got upset and started to cry.

"That night, when Dad got home, Mom told him the story. I will never forget what happened next.

"He came into my room and sat on the bed next to me. He asked me to hold out my hand, which

I did. He placed a penny in my hand and told me to close my fist around it, and to be sure that I didn't let go, no matter what.

"I closed my hand as tightly as I could, and he tried to pry my fingers open to get my penny. I squeezed even harder – no way was I going to let go of my money!

"Then Dad did something I never expected. He reached in his pocket and pulled out a ten-dollar bill. Ten dollars! He folded it, and after reminding me not to open my hand for any reason, he began trying to fit the bill into my fist. He tried and tried, but my hand was closed so tightly that there was no way for the ten dollars to fit into my fist.

"After a minute he said, 'Son, when we hold on too tightly to the things that we think are ours, it is hard for God to give us more. Just like you a minute ago. You were holding on so tight to the penny that you couldn't receive the ten dollars.

"Remember this always – a closed heart is closed both ways. You may not give anything, but you won't be able to receive anything either.' He got up and left the room.

"I thought about what he said. I went and got the toy that Judy wanted to play with, and I took it to her room. That night, I gave her my toy – not just to play with. I gave it to her to keep.

Sid reached in his shirt, and pulled out a penny hung on a fine sterling silver chain. He looked at it for a long moment and said, "Here is that penny. I have kept it all these years. I carry it with me everywhere. And whenever I feel selfish, I remember the penny."

A note to you, gentle reader. I wrote this story originally for my book "The Boss" but it continues to resonates with me over the years.

Remember the penny.

-The Penny, excerpt from *The Boss* by Terry D. Newberry

THE SHOES

Dean was a high schooler working for a fast-food joint that sold burgers and chicken and such. It was a local hangout and Dean loved working there.

His boss had taught him so much about work ethic, mindset and his approach to life in general. Dean was a foster kid and absorbed these life lessons from eagerly from the man he affectionately called The Boss.

The Boss had noticed Dean's mindset and how hard he worked, and continued to mentor him.

One day, the Boss said to Dean, "I wonder if you can help me with something."

Dean looked at the Boss. "Sure, anything. What do you need?"

"Next week is Sid Jr.'s birthday, and I wanted to get him a gift. I was thinking about a nice pair of dress shoes. But I don't know what style he would like. So, I thought maybe you could help me pick a style."

Sid Jr. was The Boss's son, who also worked at the restaurant.

"Sure, I can do that. No problem," replied Dean.

"OK, then," said the Boss. "Let's go!"

Dean followed the Boss to his car. It was a big red Ford Station Wagon they used when they catered events. It smelled just like the inside of the restaurant; a mixed aroma of fried chicken, grease, salt and grilled onions that Dean had come to associate with his home away from home.

On the way to the shoe store, Dean took the opportunity to learn more about the Boss. Dean found out that he came from a large family, and had spent most of his life working. He never finished high school, because he had to drop out in order to work and help support his brothers and sisters. But as soon as he was able, he got his GED.

He worked at a large industrial bakery for nearly his entire life, rising well before dawn and often not arriving back home until after dark. When the opportunity to open his first restaurant came along, he thought long and hard about the risk and potential rewards. He and his wife had seven children, most of who were still living at home, so the stakes were high.

"Looking back on it, my only regret is that I didn't strike out on my own sooner," he said. "I always worked hard when I worked for someone else, but I work extra hard in my own business.

The restaurants have provided not only financial reward, they have also allowed me to help a lot of people along the way. And I am grateful for the chance to work with the great team we have."

Dean thought about the life The Boss had lived. He had overcome many obstacles to become successful. Along the way, he had maintained a heart geared toward helping others. It was a potent mix in Dean's estimation. And he thought, not for the first time, that he would like to become such a person.

They arrived at the shoe store, and the Boss told the sales clerk, "I am looking for some dress shoes with good arch support and non-slip soles and heels. They should be durable and easy to clean. He will help us choose the style," he said, nodding toward Dean.

The clerk showed them five or six pairs of shoes that met the Boss's requirements. Dean looked at each pair, and finally decided on a snazzy black dress loafer that he thought Sid would love to wear.

It was the kind of shoe that Dean would have liked to own, but there wasn't much of a chance for that to happen. He owned exactly one pair of shoes, and he was wearing them.

Dean had been in foster care since he was five. As a foster child, each year he received a one-time clothing allowance. If he outgrew or wore out his clothing in the 12-month interim between allowances, well, that was just life. He always assumed that everyone was like him.

But he learned the difference one day when he went to a friend's house. He remembered that day vividly. It was a cool, crisp autumn day, the leaves on the trees a kaleidoscope of reds and yellows and browns. It was a fine day to be alive.

He arrived at his friend's house, and knocked on the door. "Hey, wanna play football?" he asked as his buddy Jerry stepped outside.

"Sure! Let's play!" Jerry replied.

Dean said, "Ok, I'll wait here for you to change into your play clothes."

Jerry looked at him oddly. "These are my play clothes."

Dean looked at his friend, who was dressed in what appeared to be brand-new jeans, clean white Converse tennis shoes, and a really nice button-down cotton shirt. Jerry's play clothes were much nicer than his own Sunday best wardrobe. For the first time, he thought that maybe he was different from the other kids at school.

That realization hit home later that same year, when he was around eight or nine years old. It was nearing the time when he would get his annual clothing allowance from the State Welfare Office.

The sole of one of his old tennis shoes had come loose, and flopped as he walked down the school hall, echoing off the lockers and bulletin boards. He had tried to mend it, first with masking tape, and when that failed, with electrical tape. But nothing worked. *Slap-flop, slap-flop, slap-flop...* every kid in school knew Dean was coming down the hall. He remembered the jeers and laughter in the lunchroom as kids yelled out, "Watch out! Here comes old Dean Slap-Flop!"

Dean got a new clothing allowance and new shoes shortly after that. But the nickname persisted, much to his shame.

"So, Dean, is this the pair you think Sid will like?" the Boss's question pulled him back to the present.

"Sorry? Oh, yes sir," Dean said, shaking off the cobweb of old memories. "I think he will really like them. And he will definitely look sharp!"

"I wonder what they will look like when he is wearing them?" the Boss asked. "Say," he said to the clerk, as though the idea had just hit him, "let's see how they will look when they are actually on someone's feet. Dean, what shoe size do you wear?"

"Uh… size 9 I think," said Dean.

"OK, do you have a size 9?" he asked the clerk.

"Yes sir, I will bring them right out."

Dean sat on one of the chairs lining the isle between racks of shoes. The clerk brought the shoes from the storage room at the back of the store. As he opened the box, Dean could smell the good smells of leather and shoe polish.

He pulled off his worn tennis shoe, and the clerk used a shoehorn to slip the loafer onto his foot. "Let's see both on," said the Boss.

"Yes sir," replied the clerk, as he put the other shoe on Dean's foot.

"Dean, walk down the aisle a bit and let's see how they look," said the Boss.

Dean walked to the end of the aisle, and back again. He marveled at how good the shoes felt on his feet. The leather wrapped around each foot and seemed to cradle it. The cushioned leather arch support made him feel taller. Dean remembered his summer job at the courthouse, and those sharply dressed attorneys coming up the court steps. He imagined they must have worn shoes like this.

"We'll take them," declared the Boss.

Dean looked at him. "Wow, that's weird. I didn't know Sid and I wore the same shoe size."

"You don't son," the Boss replied. "These are for you. I noticed that you wear those tennis shoes to work every day. You spend a lot of time on your feet, and those don't give you very good support. I don't want you to develop foot problems. You're part of my family now."

"But Boss, I can't afford these!" Dean cried, suddenly nervous.

The Boss looked at him for a long moment with a gentle smile. His gaze made Dean feel important somehow.

"But I can," he said.

Dean was quiet on the ride back to the restaurant. He had no words to describe what had just transpired. Never in his life had anything even remotely like that ever happened. No one, not even his parents on the rare occasions that he saw them, had ever done such an extravagant thing.

It wasn't about the money, although Dean was sure the shoes were expensive. It was about the fact that the Boss had noticed his lack of shoes, and had taken the interest and time from his busy life to take him and buy shoes for him.

The Boss seemed to understand his quiet reflection, and didn't say much on the ride back either.

But as they parked and got out of the car, he said, "Dean, I am proud of you and how hard you work. You will make a tremendous mark on the world one day."

And although Dean loved the gift of the shoes, it paled in comparison to that simple declaration of faith made by a man he admired.

-The Shoes, excerpt from *The Boss* by Terry D. Newberry

Afterword

This project started a little over a year ago. We were all stuck at home, couldn't go anywhere, watching the world implode around us. I was talking to friends who were feeling a little... overwhelmed. I was feeling overwhelmed myself. So, I did what usually do when life gets to be little much.

I prayed.

I asked my heavenly Dad for a sense of peace. I wrote about that in the short story called "Fireflies". I posted it on Facebook and I began to get notes and calls from folks saying how much it had lifted their spirits. They asked if maybe I could write something else.

Well, I figured perhaps I could write a piece or two to get us all through what we believed would be a month or so of isolation.

So, I put another couple of tales out there, and again, got responses asking for another story where those came from.

Another month came and went. Shortages continued. Still no meat. Still no flour. Still no paper towels. Still no toilet paper. Still no Lysol. Still no end in sight.

A lot of shortages, but one thing which was not in short supply was worry. Anxiety. Despair even.

Fires in our streets. Roving bands of marauders destroying everything in their path. Mayhem and madness. Pictures on the wire of our cities burned and decimated, looking like something from the six o'clock news about war-torn Beirut or Afghanistan.

So, I wrote another story. Something to help us remember the good things. Something to remind us that we were in a dark time, but the light would return.

The weeks tolled past, and the stories kept coming. Just when I thought I was done and the well of words had dried up, my muse would show up and inspire new ones.

And folks began asking about a book. Hey Terry! These are great, you should put them in a book, they said. We would definitely buy such a book, they said. It'll be fun they said.

I thought about it and started a project to do just that. The working title was *The Quarantine Letters*.

I've published a couple of books, but this new one is unlike anything I've written before. It is a collection of short stories from my heart to the heart of you, gentle reader. It was birthed from a desire to remind myself and others of the beauty of life and friendship and love…and the love our heavenly Dad has for us.

The stories range from remembrances of childhood to the experience of raising children of my own. They remind us of simpler times, of gentler times. They remind us of the important things. They remind us that no matter how dark our surroundings may be, there is a light within us that will banish darkness.

The darkest night cannot withstand the light from a single flame.

There was a time when things seemed to move a little slower. When the world didn't seem quite so hectic and there was room for the important things.

When peace was a little easier to come by, and there was time for visiting on the front porch swing.

A time of daughters dancing on the tops of daddy's feet, and daddies teaching their sons to hit a baseball.

A time of simple pleasures; of books and music and the kindness of strangers.

It was a more innocent time, when we walked in step with the backbeat and static coming from old AM radios. *Backbeats and Innocence* is about those times.

Fast forward fourteen months. A ton of stories have been written. More and more questions about a book have been received and answered. And now it is here.

I want to thank all of you who kept asking about the book. Your calls and letters kept the idea going. I want to thank each of you who read these stories and carried away a tiny bit of the light they offered.

And most of all, I want to thank my muse. For the inspiration and encouragement.

One beat at a time.

Special Thanks –

To Nan for putting up with the endless hours I holed myself away in my study, puzzling out the random words that eventually found their way into these pages.

To Ashlee and Amanda and Jon and Mason – you guys do it right. You inspire me.

To Tricia, who told me I should do this book and chastised me for taking so long.

Special thanks and appreciation to all the friends, mentors, and leaders who helped me recognize and walk around the potholes of life and who show up in these stories.

To the amazing Calvin Miller, for his constant encouragement to a young(ish) writer. I know your homecoming was sweet.

Thank you to you, dear reader for support well remembered and deeply appreciated.

To my heavenly Dad for never giving up on me. Ever.

Terry D. Newberry
Atlanta, Georgia
May 1, 2021
Imagine the possibilities...

About the Author

Terry D. Newberry is an author and speaker. He currently lives in Atlanta with his wife, his books, his drum set and a cat.

He still listens to vinyl records.

For additional information, go to terrynewberry.com

PSALM/**one** PRESS